# DAYDREAMS ON VIDEO

*I can't tell you a single thing about the Red Ribbon gig. I felt as if I were in a glass bubble of my own, floating miles above everybody: blissfully happy. This time tomorrow, I am going to be in love...*

# Daydreams on Video

# Adèle Geras

Hodder and Stoughton

For Julia Eccleshare

This collection
copyright © 1989, Adèle
Geras

This collection first published
in Great Britain in 1989 by
Lightning

DAYDREAMS ON VIDEO first
published in *Electric Heroes,*
edited by Mick Gowar, The
Bodley Head, London 1988.
BALLOONS first published in
*Just Seventeen* (July/August
1985).
VAMP TILL READY OR
ZULEIKA WHO? first published
by Lightning, 1989.
PLAIN MISS first published in
*Woman's Own,* March 1985.
WE'LL MEET AGAIN first
published in *Beware! Beware!,*
edited by Jean Richardson,
Hamish Hamilton, London
1987.
TWELVE HOURS –
NARRATIVE AND
PERSPECTIVES first published
in *More to life than Mr. Right,*
edited by Rosemary Stones,
Piccadilly Press, London 1985.
SNAPSHOTS OF PARADISE
first published in *Snapshots of
Paradise* by Adèle Geras,
Atheneum, New York 1983.

**British Library CIP**

Geras, Adèle
  Daydreams on video.
  I. Title
  823'.914 [F]

ISBN 0-340-51255-5

Printed and bound in Great
Britain for Hodder and Stoughton
Paperbacks, a division of Hodder
and Stoughton Ltd., Mill Road,
Dunton Green, Sevenoaks, Kent
TN13 2YA, (Editorial Office: 47
Bedford Square, London, WC1B
3DP) by Cox & Wyman Ltd.,
Reading.

# Contents

# DAYDREAMS
# ON VIDEO

## 8th December

There was a time, I'm told (though I find it quite hard to believe), when you just listened to music. Or danced to it. Or sat through open-air concerts with it wafting all around you, while you concentrated on love and peace. In any case videos didn't exist. I know this because I come from a long line of 100%, bona fide, copper-bottomed, guaranteed pure Ravers of one kind and another. Well, perhaps not so much a long line as a very noisy and articulate one. With views on subjects like Early Bob Dylan, mid-Seventies Rolling Stones albums, Cajun influences on Country and Western music, the Beatles, Elvis, Emmy Lou Harris, U2, the Eurythmics... You name it, someone in our family goes for it in a big way. My parents were young in the Sixties, which probably accounts for it. They feel a sense of personal achievement when Paul McCartney or David Bowie appears on TV.

'Still looks pretty good,' my Dad says approvingly, and pulls his stomach in. 'Sounds pretty good, too.'

My Mum scoffs at some of the stuff she has to sit through on Top of the Pops. But when we accuse her or Dad of being old-fashioned, she points out that most of the albums in the house were bought by them and not us.

9

'Us' is me, my big sister Manda, who's seventeen and my younger brother, Joey. Joey likes the latest – doesn't matter what it is. If it's in the charts, or better still, on the cover of No. 1, he'll like it. Still, he's only ten, so he'll learn. Manda is what *Smash Hits* calls 'a wannabee'. At the moment, she wants to be Madonna ('a Madonna wannabee') but Madonna has changed her style so often that poor old Manda's practically giddy from trying to keep up with the shifting kaleidoscope of hair, jewels, dresses and knick-knacks. Life was much simpler when she was an Annie Lennox wannabee. She dyed her hair orange, then had most of it cut off, and bought a pin-striped suit from Oxfam. I don't wannabee anybody, but recently I have been drawn towards the Gothic. Not the music so much, more the pale face and black this-n-thats draped about all over the place. You can cover up a lot of yourself with black hanging thingies, and if I'm to be honest, I'm nearer to being fat than to being thin.

I'm a Red Ribbon fan. I'm a Red Ribbon maniac, as a matter of fact. You've probably never heard of them, as they're quite new, but believe me when I tell you they're the greatest thing since Iron Filings (and they were pretty terrific), I'm sure you'll agree. What I like about Red Ribbon is their singer, Hilly Thomas. Hilly is short for Hilary. She's large. Not fat exactly, but big and solid with a voice that goes through you and round you and lifts you up and strokes you and kisses you and cuts you up a bit and leaves you crying. They've had a couple of songs in the lower reaches of the charts and an interview in *Smash Hits*, so when I heard

10

they were playing the Apollo in December, I wasn't taking any chances about tickets. Booking opened on June 5th, at 8.00 a.m. at the Box Office. I began my campaign on June 2nd at breakfast:

*Me*: 'I'm going to have to get up dead early on Friday.'

*Mum*: 'Why's that, then?'

*Me*: 'I'm cycling down to the Apollo, queuing for tickets for Red Ribbon.'

*Dad*: 'What about school, then?'

*Me*: 'I'll cycle to school after I've got my ticket. Janice's going too. It's not just me.'

*Joey*: 'What do you call early? I bet it's not really early.'

*Me* (nonchalantly): 'Five o'clock, I thought. To be there, that is. Leave here at about twenty to.'

*Mum* (voice rising half an octave): 'But that's the middle of the night...'

*Dad*: 'And who do you think will cook you breakfast?'

*Me*: 'I don't need breakfast cooked for me. I am fourteen, for heaven's sake... I won't disturb anyone.'

*Mum*: 'You'd better not...' (sighing) 'I suppose it's all right... some kids have paper rounds...'

*Dad*: 'But not Cass. She's never been able to get up in the morning.'

*Me*: 'I will for Red Ribbon.'

*Joey*: 'I wouldn't. She's a fat old bag, that Hilly.'

*Me* (rising high, high above that remark and keeping my hands from closing around my brother's neck): 'Coming from someone as illiterate as you about the whole spectrum of pop music,' (I

11

liked that word, spectrum, and I could tell Joey didn't know what it meant) 'such insults mean nothing. Less than nothing. Pass the Sugar Puffs.'

At this point, Manda came into the kitchen and we fell silent, taking in the look of the moment.

I spent the next day and a half packing and unpacking stuff into my school bag. I wanted to be sure I had everything. Food supplies: two packets of crisps, and some peanuts and a couple of tubes of fruit gums. A kagoule in case it rained. A cushion to sit on – well, I'd be there for three hours. Janice was bringing a radio. I put in a packet of Kleenex. I thought about taking a book, then decided against it. Clothes was the biggest problem. School uniform had to be rolled up and put in the bicycle basket for changing into. What I was wearing had to be warm, comfortable, old (we'd probably be sitting on the pavement) and fantastically glamorous, just in case. Just in case what? Well, just in case SOMEONE happened to pitch up in the queue. And who is Someone, I can hear you asking. I didn't know at that point, did I? Because I hadn't met him yet, but I was convinced that one day, somehow, somewhere, there he'd be. It's the fault of the videos. I'm always imagining I'm in one, and the kind of video it is depends very much on the mood I'm in. For instance, while I was trying on outfits in front of my mirror, deciding what to wear, I felt like the 'Sledgehammer' video, where Peter Gabriel's head keeps changing from one thing to another so quickly that the eye has trouble taking it all in. When I'm depressed, I'm in one of those black and white pouring-with-rain-in-the-city scenes, saxaphones wailing on the soundtrack and coat collars turned up as far as they'll go. And before 5th June, whenever I thought of this Someone (which I did quite a lot, feeling at times that perhaps I'd never meet anyone to fall in love with) I imagined myself in one of those fuzzy, pastel coloured films which look more like shampoo advertisements than anything else.

But it wasn't in the least like that. It's now 8th December. The Red Ribbon gig is tomorrow. Between 5th June and now, I've run and rerun the film of everything that happened that morning so many times... if it had been a real film and not just one in my head, it would have worn out entirely by now. Tomorrow night... I'll run the memory through again, just once more... only once more... honestly.

Picture the scene. A June dawn, or a little way past it, in a teenager's bedroom. I can't turn the light on and wake Manda, so I have to pick my way through a minefield of bangles and high-heeled shoes and over a couple of small hillocks of books. OK, they're my books and I'm the one who should have put them back on the shelves last night... I know, I know, but all my remorse doesn't help when the sharp corner of a particularly hard hardback catches me in the fleshiest part of my shin. Nevertheless, I manage to get dressed and out of there without waking my sister, congratulating myself on my efficiency in leaving all my gear for school and queue in a neat bundle beside the back door.

I looked out of the kitchen window while I ate my muesli. It had rained during the night, and all the early birds were actually out pulling worms from in amongst the daisies on our lawn. It gave me a real kick to see a proverb taking place before my eyes. I half expected to see the pink worm stretched in a long, elasticated line from grass to beak, like in a cartoon. But those birds didn't have to pull at all: sucked the poor things out, it seemed, like so many strands of spaghetti. This spectacle took my mind off my muesli, which tastes like wood shavings anyway and which I only eat out of guilt. The rest of the day I'm usually stuffing my face with all manner of lethal stuff, so I like to start out feeling worthy and virtuous – it's like a punishment in advance.

Anyway, off I set eventually, through the sleeping streets. Places look different early in the morning, and this was an especially soft, pink, windless sort of morning, which blurred the edges of tower blocks in a kind of mist. The sunlight gave an apricot glaze to every plate glass it touched. I imagined an invisible camera following me down the silky grey ribbons of roads and as there was nobody awake yet (not counting the shiny blue and white milk floats and the odd orange and white bus) I sang the whole of 'Raindrops keep falling on my head'. Have you noticed that certain kinds of weather or situations have songs all ready to sing in them, from different movies? 'Raindrops' is cycling music because of 'Butch Cassidy and the Sundance Kid' and rain (which we get a lot of up here) is, of course, Gene Kelly in 'Singing in the Rain'. I'm always astonished to see that no one is leaping and splashing in puddles. I have to keep my hands firmly in my pockets to stop them from reaching out for the nearest lamppost to twirl around. I keep my hands down and sing the words under my breath. Probably everyone else is doing that as well. It's quite a thought.

I reckoned I'd be the first person at the Apollo, or one of the first, but there were at least fifty people there when I arrived. Some of them looked as though they'd been sitting there all night. Sleeping bags were unrolled all over the pavement, some people had ghetto-blasters blasting, others had Walkmans (or 'Walkpersons' as my Dad calls them, dead non-sexist, tee hee!) and were rocking to their own unheard beat. Some people were quite openly lying down. Others were sitting cross-legged on spread-out sheets of newspaper, and a few looked as if the tide had washed them up against the side of the building and left them there like oil-slicks. About half way down the queue, I found Janice:

*Me*: 'Hi! Whatever time did you get up?'
*Janice*: 'About four. I live nearer than you.'
*Me*: 'Can I come and sit down, then? You look dead cosy, I must say.'

Janice is one of those people – I'm sure you know the kind I mean – who make a place comfy and home-like just by being there. She had an old duvet folded in half so that it looked like a settee, a thermos flask, and a little basket with a red and white checked tea towel spread over it, just like the one Red Riding Hood takes to her Granny. Honestly ... in a queue for tickets to a Red Ribbon gig!

*Janice*: 'Well, come and sit down then. It's still more than two hours till they open the Box Office.'

I sat down beside her and had a cup of tea and a chocolate digestive or two. The muesli was three miles ago, remember? Then we started chatting which meant, if you'll forgive the frankness, discussing the boys all round us in the queue with a view to possible romance, and criticising a few of the girls as well, as we went along: their hair, earrings, tights, shoes, and the way they were sitting/standing/lying down or whatever. After about an hour of this, we came to the conclusion that the queue was low on heart-throbs and the pavement rather hard on our bottoms, even through the duvet.

*Me*: 'What're you going to do with this duvet? You're not bringing it to school, are you?'
*Janice*: 'I'm taking it home. You can come too and change at my house. We ought to be able to get to school before nine.'
*Me*: 'Unfortunately. Give me another choccy bic, then.'

So it went on. I thought it would be interesting being in a queue, seeing all the different types of people, but it was boring. Nobody was properly dressed up. Nobody had bothered because it was so early in the morning, I suppose, but they all looked dead ordinary: scruffy and sleepy and fed-up. In jeans and dirty trainers for the most part, all their fine feathers folded up at home in their chests of drawers.

I was almost wishing I'd brought my book to read when I saw him. It was nearly eight o'clock, only a few minutes before the Box Office opened. He'd arrived at a time when the queue stretched right round the building. The first thing I thought when I saw him was: he's a wannabee as well. He's just like that Ben Vol-au-Vent Asparagus Tips, as *Smash Hits* calls him, from Curiosity Killed the Cat. He had approached the queue from our end and stopped beside us, looking down the seemingly endless line of bodies disappearing into the distance. He sighed. I could see his shoulders droop under his grey sweatshirt. The lace on his right trainer had come undone. He was biting his lip, I could see that he was trying very hard not to cry.

I don't know exactly what made me do what I did next. It just struck me all at once as a brilliant idea. I said, in a very loud voice so that everyone around could hear me:

'There's our Joey! Blimey, he's taken his time getting here...' I was pinching Janice while I said this, so she realized something was up. She very sensibly said nothing and buried her face in the basket, looking for something to eat. Meanwhile, I ran up to this lad, grabbed him by the arm and shouted loudly about him being a dozy so and so and better late than never. The boy looked as if I were a ten ton truck bearing down on him. Luckily, he didn't run away. I said, through clenched teeth and in a whisper:

'Give us your money and I'll get you a ticket when I get ours. They'll all be sold if you join the end of the line. Meet us over there afterwards.' I nodded my head towards the bus shelter across the street. He opened his mouth to speak, but I wouldn't let him. 'I won't run away with your money, you know . . . Look, you can hold on to this.' I picked up my basket (school uniform, books, kagoule, etc) and gave it to him. Perhaps I was no longer a ten ton truck. Perhaps I was more like some kind of hypnotist. I found myself suddenly standing very close to him, hiding with my body the fact that he was giving me a £10 note.

'Thanks,' he said. 'You didn't have to do that . . . it's really kind.'

'You go and wait over at the bus stop,' I said. 'You can watch us going right up into the Box Office.'

He nodded and shambled over to sit on the bench in the bus shelter, clutching all my stuff. I went back to Janice's duvet, shaking all over.

*Janice:*: 'Whatever's got into you? Who was that?'

*Me*: 'I don't know. I never saw him before in my life.'

*Janice*: 'You never . . . I don't know. You're crazy, you know that? Quite crazy.'

*Me*: 'Why? I could see he was upset, that's all . . . disappointed, I decided to help him. I don't know why that's so terrible.'

*Janice*: 'Well, you know nothing at all about him. He may be a junkie or a mugger . . .'

*Me*: ' . . . or a child molester or the Wild Man of Borneo or even the Jolly Green Giant, but I don't know what the fuss is about. I'm only buying him a ticket, for heaven's sake. I'm not bloody marrying him.'

*Janice*: 'Tsk! Tsk! Temper, temper. I haven't said a word... I take it all back. Have another chocolate digestive.'

I couldn't even eat. That shows, better than anything, what had happened. I had been hit, struck just like in all the songs, and all the cartoons and all the jokes by an enormous great Cupid's arrow, right in my heart. I couldn't believe it. It was exactly like everybody's always singing about. One look and then my heart went boom kind of thing. All those sleepy, unwashed, pavement-stained nobodies we wouldn't have looked at twice suddenly seemed like the assembled cast of a glamorous movie, just on the point of breaking into song and moving in complicated dance routines along the street. Fanning out into the side roads and jumping in and out of traffic, like in the opening moments of 'West Side Story'. I could see him (what was his name? I didn't even know that) sitting on the bench. The distance between us felt like miles and miles. I found I could say nothing about this to Janice. The queue started moving. Do you know the bit in 'My Fair Lady' when Freddy What'sisname says he's floating about seven storeys high? I felt just like that. It's a funny thing. I'd always thought it was a bit of poetic exaggeration and it turns out to have been quite accurate. There you go: learn something new every day, don't you?

It's at this point that my memory video speeds up, becomes one of those jerky, everybody-moving-like-a-machine-out-of-control kind of things. I'm saying: 'Three in the circle, please,' and pushing money through a hole in a sheet of glass, and getting three skimpy-looking squares of pinkish paper in return. He's waiting for me when I go over. I think I nearly got killed crossing the road, but I can't really remember... Anyway, there he is, and he stands up when I hand him his ticket and he says thanks ever so much. I mutter something about his being welcome and we both stand there shifting from one foot to the other and I manage to ask where he's from. He says Rochdale and that's why he got to the queue so late, and he'd better get going 'cos he was going to be about two hours late for school and he'd get done. It was going to be a great gig, and ta once again. He didn't know, he said, what he'd have done without me – see you, he said, see you at the gig then. And off he went.

I stood there, unable somehow to get my body to work properly. My feet seemed to have become embedded in the concrete. See you at the gig. Great holes started to open up inside me when I thought of all the hours and hours and hours of time that had to pass between now and then. I thought of Time as a gigantic reel of tape, winding itself on to a spool, slowly. Not for the first time, I wished I had a Fast Forward button I could press to make the days go more quickly. And (this thought only occurred to me as I dragged my feet across to where Janice was waiting) I didn't even know his name. I couldn't even call him something to myself when I thought of him. Ben was a bit obvious, so I gave him the name Cat. That had a nice, jungly feel to it. Cat. When I got back to Janice, the conversation went something like this:

*Janice*: 'Has he gone, then?'

*Me*: 'Yeah. He's from Rochdale.'

*Janice*: 'Wouldn't have thought he'd be in such a hurry to get back, then.'

*Me*: 'Levenshulme's not exactly Monte Carlo either, is it?'

*Janice*: 'Keep your hair on. What's he called, then?'

*Me*: 'Don't know. Never asked.'

*Janice* (sighing): 'You're not half stupid, you. Come on, let's get cracking. We'll meet up with him at the gig, won't we? He'll be in the next seat. You can get acquainted properly then.'

That's it. That's number one on my personal Dream Video Chart. It's held its position for six months – a record. Tomorrow is the gig. I don't think I'll get too much sleep tonight somehow. I've been so busy the last six months imagining how it will be when we meet at the gig that I'm scared stiff now. The time has almost come. My video daydreams have kept me going, I can tell you. I can't decide which I like best. There's one where he turns up with a bunch of flowers and gives them to me without saying a word. In that one, all the racket in the background and all the people in the seats around us go fuzzy and wavy and eventually disappear altogether, leaving us staring silently into one another's eyes.

Sometimes, I like the one that has shy smiles all the way through the gig, and then a muttered: 'Can I see you home, then?' right at the end, followed by a long walk through dark streets with very shiny pavements. In this one, I'm wearing a very smart black PVC raincoat (which I haven't actually got) which is long and almost as shiny as the pavements. There's even one video daydream with suspense in it. The seat is empty. Horror of horrors. He isn't there at all. Then in the interval, in he comes, half dead, wet, mud-splattered. His bus from Rochdale broke down and he had to hitch a lift. Lorries kept driving through puddles next to him as he walked, but he simply had to come. He knew, he just knew that I'd be waiting, and that I'd spent the last six months thinking of him. He, of course, had spent every minute since June doing nothing but picturing my face.

I can't decide which daydream I like best. I can't even write any more now. I can't do anything at all until tomorrow.


## 11th December

I must write all this now, because tomorrow I've got to catch the bus to Rochdale. They say truth is stranger than fiction, and they've got a point, they have really.

I have no memory at all about getting to the Red Ribbon gig. It was lucky I was with Janice, who was taking in all the stuff her Dad was telling us about where he'd be parked after the show, etc. I was standing in the foyer, scanning every face I saw, looking for Cat. Normally what I was seeing would have kept me happy for hours: orange mohicans, dreadlocks, green spikes, white faces with black eyes like pandas, leather and chains and fur and silk and lace and embroidery and that was just the lads.

22

But there was no sign of Cat anywhere. OK, I said to myself while this carnival whirled around my head, it's the 'I'll get there through hell and high water' video that's going to come true.

By the time we went in, I was quite prepared to have an empty seat beside me, at least for the first half. What I was not prepared for was Mrs. Secretary of the Year sitting tidily in the seat that should have been Cat's. She looked really out of place. First of all, she was old: older than my mother. She was wearing a straight black skirt and a white lacy blouse, and on her lap she was holding a black bag like the ones we used to have in the dressing-up box when I was little. We wore them over our arms, pretending to be ladies. I could have hit her.

'Excuse me,' I said as I went past her to our seat. Then, as I sat down and just as I was about to launch into a speech about the seat really belonging to a friend of mine, she said:

'I'm sorry , but I think you're the girl who helped my son buy his ticket for this concert. Please excuse me if I'm wrong.'

I was totally flummoxed. This was Cat's mother, of all people. Where was Cat, then? Why wasn't he here? Why had she come? I was just going to ask all this when she said:

'He made me come. He was that unhappy, not being able to get here himself. Not so much for the concert...' (I kept wishing she wouldn't call it that. It sounded silly.) '... as, well, he wanted to see you. That's the truth of the matter. He made me come. He forced me to. He was absolutely set on it, I could see.'

'But what's wrong with him?' I managed to say at last.

'He's at home in bed. He's really quite poorly. He's had a really bad go with his throat this time, so the doctor's keeping him in bed for a few more days. He'll have to have his tonsils out when he's better. Anyway, I was to tell you all this and I was to get your name and address and to give you this. Here.' She snapped the handbag open and took out an envelope. 'He wrote you a letter.'

'What's his name?' was all that I could find to say.

'Alan. Alan Reid.'

'It's really nice of you to come. Please give Alan my (I was going to say "love") best wishes.'

'He's asked you to visit us,' she said, tapping the letter. 'Can I tell him to expect you? He did say I should try and get you to come on Saturday.'

'This Saturday?'

'Yes, the 12th. Shall I tell him you'll come? You'll be very welcome. Come and have lunch with us. He won't be able to do much entertaining, mind. Still, he'll be that pleased to see you.'

'Thank you,' I said. 'I'd love to come.'


I can't tell you a single thing about the Red Ribbon gig. I felt as if I were in a glass bubble of my own, floating miles above everybody: blissfully happy. Now here I am. I had a bit of a problem with my Mum and Dad at first. I had to tell them the whole story and then my Mum had to ring Mrs. Reid and check with her and all kinds of fusses were made about timetables and so on. Dad's giving me a lift to

24

Stockport and then I'm catching a dead romantic-sounding bus called the Trans Lancs Express. It's almost as good as the Orient Express. They've got all the places it goes to written up in the station. If you say them aloud it sounds like a song:

'Wigan-Bolton-Bury-Rochdale
Oldham-Ashton-Stockport-Airport.'

Someone should write it, make it into a hit. But it won't be me. This time tomorrow, I'm going to be in love.

# **BALLOONS**

## Part One

Whenever Gina thought about her own mind, she
pictured it as one of the glittery, heart-shaped, gas-
filled balloons sold for a quid, down on the Prom.
Her mind-balloon was pink, covered with lacy
patterns, and if you didn't keep a firm grip on it, it
would fly out into the wide sky and grow smaller
and smaller, until it was no more than a twinkle, far
away.

Gina had only one more day to go before her
holiday and she felt distinctly creative. She was
making, or rather assembling, plates of tuna fish
salad from assorted bowls of this and that which
stood on the counter of the Western Grill and
Griddle. People liked salads in hot weather. Hot
oil, greasy burgers and soggy chips could just about
be interpreted as comforting on chilly days, but in
all this heat... yuck! It turned your stomach, it did
really. Salads, well, there were possibilities. Gina
arranged a fan of tomato slices, a little three-leaf
clover of cucumber, some beige tuna flakes, a
couple of bits of beetroot and a lettuce leaf that had
seen better days, on the plate in front of her, and let
her mind slide up, up and out of the Western Grill
and Griddle, away from the bottles crusted with
blood-brown ketchup and the unswept floor to...
to the deck of a yacht in the Mediterranean...

Where Gina lay in a white bikini on a black mattress and toasted her delectable flesh in the sun, her mind in a turmoil. What to wear for the Cannes Film Festival? Was chiffon too vulgar? Silk too ostentatious? Cotton too common? Oh, God the problems, the heartaches, the indescribable sufferings associated with this gruelling life. Giving, giving... always on show. Oh, how the beautiful Gina yearned for obscurity...

The real Gina came to in a rush. Someone had asked for salad.

'I don't fancy the beetroot, though, do you, Peggy?'

'Yes, I like a bit of beetroot on mine. Nice and sharp it is, if you take my meaning.'

'Well, I don't fancy it myself. One tuna salad with beetroot and one without, Miss, please.'

'Right,' said Gina. 'Here's the one with the beetroot. If you'd like to pay at the till, I'll bring the one without to your table.'

Off they went, Peggy and her buddy. Gina knew she should design, make, create, a whole new beetroot-free salad, but what the hell. She picked up the two offending slices with a fork and ate them, then she wiped the deep pink stains from the plate with a bit of Kleenex kitchen towel, selected another lettuce leaf from the bowl and draped it as elegantly as she could to cover the space.

The afternoon trickled by. No one wanted salads any more. Soon, they'd start coming in for cups of tea and ice-creams: hot, pink flesh bubbling out of shorts, suntops, bathing suits, noses neon-lit with sunshine, eyes white-rimmed where the sun-glasses had been, and all the boys with something wrong with them. They were all skinny, or pimply, or fat, or crooked-nosed, or too pale, or too red, or too bloody something. One day why didn't someone like... like who? Like almost anyone decent-looking, that's like who, walk in here and say... There. There goes the bright balloon again, thought Gina, pull it down this minute. Stop dreaming and concentrate on the fish. Three poor little goldfish were swimming round in the really depressing fish-tank near the fruit machines at the back of the café. If it was mine, Gina thought, I'd get the shells they sell in the souvenir shops to put in it... all pink on the inside and stripy on the outside... and a model of a Spanish galleon and some frondy weeds to wave about... and I'd bloody well clean up the water, what's more. Poor little things. They can hardly see through it, it's more like soup than water. Or liquid fog.

'Could I have a coffee, d'you think?'

Gina looked up. Blinked. Was this a dream that had crept up on her while she wasn't looking? Her hand shook as she poured the coffee. He'd gone over to his table. When I turn around, Gina thought, he'll be gone. He won't be real. Or else he'll be different.

'There you are.' He was just the same. Gina thought: it shouldn't be allowed. There should be a Government Health Warning stamped on the foreheads of such boys.

'Thanks.'

'It's O.K.' She managed a smile and went quickly back behind the counter. How could she have forgotten that she was wearing the shoes that were more holes than fabric? She squinted at him from behind a basket of bread rolls. Look at the way his shirt hung in soft folds from his shoulders! Look at his brown arms . . . at the way his hair shone . . . the balloon was tugging at her wrist . . . trying to fly . . . flying . . .

' . . . I've been too shy to come in here before. I've been watching you for ages . . . come to the pictures. Come to lunch, dinner, tea, breakfast. Marry me – I can't live without you . . . Come with me . . .'

Gina crashed out of her dream as a pretty young woman asked her gently for a cup of tea. Gina liked this person quite a lot until she saw where she was going to sit. Oh, it was too much. Once in a blue moon someone nice came in here and before you could turn round, there was his girlfriend. Gina cut scones with a murderous knife and buttered them so roughly that they would have crumbled in her hands if the butter hadn't been nearly liquid anyway in the heat. I don't care, Gina said to herself. I don't care. I've got two weeks off starting tonight and I don't care. I don't have to come in here for two weeks. I'll meet someone else . . . on the beach . . . at the Fun Fair. I'll be taken over all funny on the Roller Coaster, flying away with my stomach left behind me somewhere, and he'll put an arm around me and say, 'Don't worry, just hide your eyes. We'll soon be on firm ground again. I'll take care of you . . .'

Oh, what a load of cobblers, Gina, what garbage, what complete codswallop. And now look what you've done. You've missed seeing him go . . . and he's gone. While you were feeling sorry for yourself, he's done a bunk and you'll never see him again and serve you right.

Gina moved out from behind the counter to give the tables their afternoon wipe. She ran the cloth tenderly over his table and then she saw it on the chair: a camera in a leather case. Gina knew nothing about cameras, but the case alone looked as if it would be worth a penny or two, and anyway, it was His. His. That was fate, taking a hand in no uncertain terms. She looked all over for a label, a name tag, something. Pictures filled her head: herself knocking on doors, walking up tree-lined drives, being shown into carpeted halls, ushered into drawing rooms, luxury flats, recording studios, movie studios. Anything was possible.

Nothing. No name, nothing but the label of the photographic supplies shop where he'd bought it. Gina almost wept. She knew she ought to give it to the manager, Rex, who would put it in with the plastic purses and Tricel cardigans that lived in the Lost Property Box in the kitchen... but she couldn't. She couldn't bear to part with it. No one else had seen it. She picked it up and almost ran into the cloakroom at the back of the café. There, she picked up her bag from a chair, found the most hidden corner of it, down among the used tissues and bus tickets and thrust the camera into it. As long as she had it, there was hope. Hope of seeing him again. Perhaps they'd remember at the photographic shop... who they'd sold that camera to... or she could put an ad in the paper... something. As long as she had the camera.

Sharon and Marie said: 'Lucky you, two weeks off, eh? Wish it was us. You've got the lovely weather, haven't you? We'll think of you to-morrow, lying on the beach. Lucky devil.'

Gina smiled and said nothing. Tomorrow... tomorrow, she would begin her search.


## Part Two

'Are you sitting there and seriously telling me you've lost £200 worth of camera?'

'I'm telling you it wasn't my fault!' Martin shouted.

'Then whose bloody fault was it then, eh? Tell me that!'

Bob sat down and appealed wearily to his wife. 'I ask you, Chris, honestly. Look at it from my point of view. Oh, I know he's your precious kid brother and can't put a foot wrong, but just look at my position. I give him a summer job out of the kindness of my heart, just to oblige really, I don't have to, do I? And what does he do? First day out? Loses the flaming camera, doesn't he?'

'Calm down, Bob,' said Christine. 'It wasn't really his fault. I mean, if it was his fault, then it was mine as well. I mean, I was with him...'

Martin sighed. 'You didn't know I'd put it on the chair, though, did you? You came in after me.'

'But Bob, he went straight back there this morning, didn't you Martin?'

'Yes, no one knew anything about it.'

'Clear what's happened then, isn't it?' Bob muttered. 'Someone's gone and nicked it, that's what... bloody hell, it's the last time I'm helping you out, is that clear? Have you any idea how much that camera cost? Have you? Eh?'

'I'll pay you back,' Martin said.

'How, eh? Heard of youth unemployment? Who's going to give you a job, eh? Eh? I did, as a favour to your sister. Can't think who else would be dumb enough to employ you.'

'I can't listen to any more of this,' Martin muttered. 'I'm leaving.'

'Good riddance,' shouted Bob.


Martin sat on a bench on the Prom and looked across the road at where a larger-than-life plaster figure of Grandma Clampitt sat on her rocking chair in a glass case. She was wearing a gingham dress, and held a revolver across her knees. Her blue eyes stared out icy and unseeing and her metallic voice crackled and boomed from between stiff lips:

'C'mon in to the Shooting Gallery, y'all! It sure is a whole lot 'a fun!'

The Shooting Gallery to which Grandma Clampitt was inviting everyone so warmly was the fourth place in a row which had assured Martin that 'they'd get on very nicely thank you very much' without his services. Where next? In this heat, every step was an effort. How do they do it, the trippers? How did they manage to find the energy to bounce, run about after the children, laugh, rush around funfairs, pools, on donkey rides? And how did all the girls manage to look so desirable? How was it possible that there could be all those rounded arms, velvety thighs, glossy mouths, breasts swelling and wobbling under T-shirts that said 'LOVE' and 'LIFE' and 'YES' and

'RELAX' and none of it for him? There wasn't anything wrong with him, was there? Well, there wasn't. Every time he looked into the mirror, he saw his dark eyes and shiny hair and teeth that didn't quite sparkle but that at least were miles away from yellow and all his very own. He knew that the fact he was alone had nothing to do with his looks and everything to do with his character. Too damn tongue-tied and shy. Couldn't get the right words past his lips in the right order at the right time, could he? Oh, he dreamed, of course he did. Smooth conversation-starters spilled out of him like satin ribbons:

'Where have you been all my life?'
'What are you doing for the rest of your life?'
'Do you come here often?'
'Come live with me and be my love.'
'I'm a talent scout for Virgin Records.'
'I'm a movie producer.'
'I'm a millionaire.'
'Come up and see my etchings.'
'I didn't know they made 'em like you any more.'
And soon, almost ad infinitum. It wasn't until he'd walked into the Western Grill yesterday that all his dreams had focussed on one person. The minute he'd seen her, behind the barricade where rock cakes and Danish pastries hardened on glass shelves, he'd known exactly what to do. It really had felt just like being in a movie. The rest of the café faded away like a mist and her face shone out in close up. It took all his courage to utter the words: 'Could I have a coffee, d'you think?'

(Quick someone, give him the Oscar for Screenwriting!) And as he'd floated to a table he began to work out a plan.

The camera scheme came to him with all the sparkle of a brilliant idea. He would leave his camera behind in the café and then come back and ask Gina for it. That was her name: he'd heard someone shouting from the kitchen, seen her turning to answer. She'd start talking and then it would all come out naturally, and they'd chat about photography and how his brother-in-law had given him this chance, like a kind of apprenticeship. Then he'd make her laugh as he described the funny people he'd stopped to take a picture of as they walked along in the sunshine. Then he'd tell her (it'd be easy – it'd just slip out in the conversation) what a marvellous photo he could take of her, and they'd step out into the sunshine and he'd make her smile and pout her lips and under the café overall she'd be wearing a skimpy little T-shirt... Anyway, Martin thought, shaking the dreams out of his head, there's no point pursuing that. He'd gone back this morning to discover that no one had seen or heard of his camera, and moreover that Gina had gone off for two weeks holiday, and no, they didn't know where she lived. Quite local, they thought, but they couldn't be sure. That was clearly that. Gina, let loose for two weeks in all that sun would turn golden brown and one of the slim-hipped, metal-studded glamour boys down from the big city for a bit of a giggle would sweep her off on the back of his thrusting motor-bike and into the sunset... Whatever.

Martin stood up, uncertain where to go next. Perhaps he should try the Penny Arcade. He'd avoided it the first time round because it had looked so sleazy, even in the bright sunlight, but he had £200 to pay back to Bob, didn't he? He couldn't afford to be fussy. Outside the Penny Arcade sat a laughing Clown in a glass case. This character was fed 10p bits and in return he rolled about in mirthless laughter, shiny and sharp like razor blades, laughter slicing the air all around. The clown's mouth was fixed in a solid grin. The blue paint and white paint of his eyes was crazed and cracked. It seemed to Martin that the clown was pointing at him. Look at that fool! Lost the girl, hasn't he? And where the hell does he think he's going to find £200?

## Part Three

Gina opened the door of Robert Edwards Photographic Supplies and a bell tinkled somewhere far away. She stepped into the cool shade of the shop and looked around. A tall, bearded man came in from a back room and said:

'Good morning. How can I help you?'

'Well,' Gina said. 'I don't know if you can, really. It's just . . . well, someone left a camera at the café I work at, and I wanted to find out, well, where he lived so that I could . . . you know . . . give it back. Only the label on the case says this shop.'

As Gina rummaged in her bag, the man called out:

'Chris, come in here. There's a young lady brought Martin's camera back, I think.'

Martin . . . what a lovely name . . . perhaps he'll

come in this very minute and thank her...

'Hello.' Gina looked up and blushed. It was the girlfriend. 'How lovely of you to bring the camera in... Martin'll be thrilled... it's worth £200... it's really ever so kind of you, honestly.'

'That's O.K. It's a pleasure. I could see it was expensive. It's quite all right. Truly.'

Gina walked out of the shop in a daze. Tears clouded her eyes. She felt that the whole world was shrinking round her, tightening round her like bands of steel. What right had that bloody stupid clown got to be laughing like that? What was so damn funny? Perhaps she was. That's it, she was. Pinning all her hopes on a camera, and then that girlfriend being there like that. Well, how was she supposed to know? Gina searched about in her head for a comforting dream, and couldn't find one, not now. Her mind, that pretty silver balloon, lay earthbound, lifeless, no longer shiny. The clown's laughter followed her as she walked past all the happy people, and it fell upon her ears like a maniac's wailing.

'And you let her go? Oh, God, I can't believe it. She brought the camera back and you didn't even offer her a cup of tea? I just don't know what to say.' Martin sighed.

'I'm not a mind-reader, am I?' said Chris. 'How was I supposed to know that this girl was The One? You don't exactly take people into your confidence, you know.'

'But you could have got her address. I could have written to her.'

'She'll be back in that café after her holidays, won't she?'

Martin said nothing. Didn't Chris realize what could happen in two weeks? *Who* could happen to Gina in that space of fourteen days? Pointless to explain.

'I'm going out.'

'Where?'

'I don't know. Anywhere.'

'Martin?'

'Yeah.'

'Don't be sad. You didn't even know this girl, did you? You can't be sad over someone you didn't even know, can you?'

'Guess not. 'Bye,' Martin said. You could be sad over anything. Even losing a dream by waking up in the morning was tough sometimes. Oh, Gina!

Ever since she'd been a small child, Gina had loved funfairs. They cheered her up. They made her smile. The loud music lifted her spirits. So what happened tonight? Everybody looked grotesque: too fat, too old, over made-up, like wax-works come to life. The leather jackets of the young men crackled with menace, people leered at her. The carousel horses neighed and trampled in frozen scarlet and gold, a stampede, a rush of hooves and manes and flaring nostrils. Gina fled.

The evening was turning mauve at the edges, the lights were on everywhere: pink and blue and orange and white neon strips that winked and beckoned and glittered on red, beery faces. She pushed her way through the crowds and found herself without quite knowing how, sitting at a table in the Western Grill and Griddle. Sharon was going to bring her a frothy coffee. The fish gazed at her through the murky water, moving their mouths, swishing transparent tails. Sharon hadn't wiped the table properly...

'Excuse me, is anybody sitting here?' Gina looked up. There he was. Martin.

'No. I mean, no, really, no one is.'

'D'you mind if I do?'

'No... please do.'

This is definitely a dream, Gina said to herself. This is for sure happening somewhere in the upper part of my head...

'It was good of you to bring back the camera.'

'That's O.K. Your... I mean, the lady said it was worth a lot of money.'

'Oh, it is. It's my sister. I mean, she is. It's my brother-in-law's shop. I'm supposed to take pictures of the day trippers.'

'Your sister? Are you sure?' (Oh, Gina, what a bloody silly thing to say...)

Martin started laughing. 'Yes, I'm quite sure. What does it matter?'

'No, no it doesn't, only I thought...'

'What? What did you think?'

Gina looked down. Her coffee had lost its froth. Where had that come from? Had Sharon brought it, right in the middle of this dream?

'Doesn't matter. She's pretty, isn't she?'

'Who, my sister?' (Say it, Martin, say it, quick before the chance slips away. Say it NOW, damn it!)

'She's not nearly as pretty as you are.'

41

Gina looked up. 'Will you do me a favour?'

'Anything.'

'Pinch me.'

'What?' Martin smiled.

'Go on.'

'O.K.' Martin pinched her arm gently.

Gina laughed. 'You're still here.'

''Fraid so.'

'My coffee's all cold.'

'Come for a walk.'

As we go out, Martin thought, I'll just put my arm around her shoulders... it'll be easy... everything will be easy from now on.


They stepped out together into the strip-lit darkness. Grandma Clampitt's voice echoed after them:

'... it sure is a whole lot 'a fun...'

# VAMP TILL READY
## OR
# ZULEIKA WHO?

## Second Week: Friday

Maddy Cameron is in love. Also, she didn't go to bed at all last night, but spent the dark hours backstage at the Playhouse, fitting giant plugs on to thick, black cables, and making cups of disgusting coffee in the Green Room for Ben. And others too, of course, but mainly for Ben because she loves him. Spending the night in his company, helping 'fit-up' the theatre for today's dress rehearsal of *The Importance of Being Earnest* was nothing but the purest pleasure. She remembers smiles, looks, rufflings of hair, and a kiss that meant, surely, something? Maddy is walking on air, floating along towards the Kemp in a daze: elated, excited, a little removed from reality, feverish and slightly tipsy from a potent combination of love and lack of sleep.

*Oxford.* Towers and domes and spires, grey and honey coloured stone, façades of perfect symmetry, the sound of bells in a mist that will perhaps lift later, or perhaps not. Cardigans on display at Marks and Spencer, iced cakes on shelves in the Cadena, models of country gentlewomen in tweeds in the windows of Elliston's – Maddy is oblivious to them all. She is wondering: will he be there yet, and imagines him sitting, waiting for her, pushing a lock of dark hair impatiently away from his eyes.

Maddy and Ben, Bruce and Vikki, Pete and Anna were squashed together around one small table. Ben was ordering for everyone. Rose, the elderly waitress stood quietly through what she privately thought of as 'the shenanigans'. The order would come in the end. 'Stay with me with pots of tea, comfort me with cinnamon toast,' said Ben. 'For I am sick of love, dear Rose.'

'Tea and cinnamon toast for six, then, is it?' Rose sighed.

'That's right.' Ben sat back in his chair. Maddy, sitting next to him, wondered whether she was glowing on the outside as well as on the inside. Everyone could see they were a couple, a pair. Ben had his arm around her. Every so often, in the middle of a conversation he stopped and kissed her ear, or twisted up the heavy strands of her hair in his hand, absentmindedly, as though he'd been doing it for years. The cinnamon toast arrived. Ben and Maddy fed each other small sweet pieces of it.

'Eating,' said Ben 'is frightfully erotic.' They finished the toast.

'Now that you've stopped that disgusting display of greed and passion,' said Pete 'can we talk about "Summer Salad"?'

'Yes, Ben. Come on, tell us about the show,' said Vikki. 'I don't think much of the name.' Vikki was tall and skinny, sharp-featured and freckled. I could make something of her, thought Maddy, imagining black crepe and upswept hair. Why does she always wear shapeless brown garments? Pete's

46

been going out with her for ages. He's not bad, if you like tweedy types. Not bad, but not Ben.

'The show,' Ben leaned forward, 'will be like nothing else that's been around here before. I mean, it's 1966 after all. We've had satire: "Beyond the Fringe" and your biting political stuff. I want this show to have' – he paused dramatically – 'PIZAZZ.'

'That sounds like a better name,' Vikki said. '"Pizazz with everything", or "All that Pizazz".'

'Or even,' said Ben '"Look Back in Pizazz" or "A Midsummer Night's Pizazz."'

'Sounds great,' said Bruce 'but what the hell is it?'

'Oh, I don't know,' said Ben 'Glamour, zing, oomph, sex-appeal, bounce – they're all part of it. But there's more.'

'Glamour,' said Anna, pushing her glasses further up her nose. 'I know what that means.' She laughed. 'Us ladies in scanty garments with sequins on. "Tits and teeth" I believe they say, don't they? There's only two of us, you know. Are we supposed to provide all the glamour? It's a tall order. I should bring the house down in fishnet tights.'

'Oh, Anna, how could you?' Ben grinned at her. 'We have to have a "chanteuse" don't we? And you're the tops. Maddy here is doing wardrobe, and by the time she's finished with you, you won't recognize yourself. Ethel Merman and Edith Piaf all rolled into one.'

'Rolled is right,' said Anna. 'I reckon two Mermans and two Piafs would have trouble making one of me.'

Bruce stroked Anna's hand. 'Don't be silly, love.

47

Anyone would think you were fat.'

'I am fat,' said Anna.

'No, plump,' said Ben. 'Curvaceous, luscious, sexy.'

Anna snorted. 'An amazing percentage of what you talk, Ben Ashworth, is rubbish. But who can resist those sky-blue eyes? For you, I'll cover myself in spangles and sing anything from "Home Sweet Home" to the "Halleluia Chorus".'

'You'll be lovely,' Bruce kissed her. 'Can we have a duet, Ben?'

'I'll talk to Graham and Oliver,' said Ben. 'Oliver did say something about a send-up of Nelson Eddy and Jeanette Macdonald.' He began to sing:

'"When I'm calling you... oooo... ooo,
Will you answer too... oooo... ooo?"'

People at nearby tables applauded.

'Who else have we got?' asked Pete.

'Ronny and Sam and Jack, and you four. That makes seven. And I'm holding auditions today to find one other lady.'

'She'd better be a beauty,' said Vikki. 'Anna and I are O.K. as far as we go, but we don't go all that far.'

'Any idea of what you want for a set?' asked Bruce.

'Mike Ramsden's doing it,' said Ben. 'I want it to be functional. And exciting. Possibly a revolve, or something like that. It's got to have...'

'I can guess,' said Maddy. 'Pizazz.'

'God.' said Ben. 'Auditions are hell. One poor girl after another. And I have to be so hard-hearted.

48

How much longer is this going on? How many more out there?'

Oliver, musical director for the revue, said: 'That's it. We've seen them all.'

Graham, who wrote lyrics for Oliver's songs, sighed: 'I feel as if we've seen the entire female population of Oxford.'

There was a knock on the door. Ben put his head down on the table. 'If it's not Sophia Loren or Raquel Welch or Jeanne Moreau, I don't want to know.'

'Come in,' Oliver shouted.

A voice purred: 'Am I too late?'

'No...' Ben sighed 'it's O.K.' He looked up. 'Wow,' he breathed, 'and again I say, Wow!' He blinked. 'Could you give me your name, please?'

'Leonie Mitchell.' Throatily.

'Most appropriate. You do look somewhat... leonine.'

'May I sit down?'

The vision sat down, and crossed a pair of legs that seemed to go on for yards before disappearing under a tiny skirt of soft brown suede. She arranged a cardigan over shoulders that would turn out surely, Ben thought, to be creamy: creamily white and rounded under the silky blouse. He looked at Oliver and Graham. They sat with open mouths. Stunned.

'I think,' Ben said 'that we can offer you a part in the show. Don't you agree Graham? Oliver?'

'Yes.' Graham sounded as though he had been holding his breath. Perhaps he had. Oliver nodded.

'I don't know if I'm eligible, really,' said Leonie. 'I'm only in Oxford for a bit, and I've never done anything like this before, only I would love to. I've never sung or danced before, I mean.'

'You are,' said Ben 'the very acme and zenith of eligibility, and I'm sure we can teach you.'

Leonie shook her head and a mane of gold and russet and chestnut hair fell over the curve of her cheek.

'I'd love it if you could teach me,' she said, lingering a little on 'you', and directing the beam of her smoky eyes at Ben.

'It's a deal,' he said, and had a sudden day dream of himself and Leonie whirling around on an empty stage. Himself in black, a Gene Kelly figure, and she in shreds of chiffon that did not overtax the imagination. He pulled himself together.

'The first rehearsal is on Monday. Ten o'clock. St. Margaret's Church Hall, St. Margaret's Road. Do you know it?'

'I expect I shall find it.'

'I could pick you up,' said Graham. Damn, thought Ben, why didn't I think of that? Stop, stop, he said to himself. There's Maddy. Think of Maddy, how smashing she is, what fun...

'Lovely,' said Leonie. 'Thank you. I live at 132, Walton Street. I'm longing to start.' She glided to the door. 'Goodbye.'

'Bye,' said Ben, thinking that if life really imitated art, as Oscar Wilde so stoutly maintained, he would have a nice, stiff shirt cuff to write down her address. 132, Walton Street, ho hum and a hey, nonny no!

## Sunday

'Maddy says,' said Anna, 'that Ben sounds like a second-rate Elizabethan poet when he describes her. Lips like dewy roses, hair like gold, eyes like the firmament, all that sort of thing.'

'A walking cliché,' Vikki nodded, buttering another piece of toast. 'I'm quite curious to see her, I must say.'

'I'm not,' Anna was lying on her bed. 'I think she sounds like that what's-her-name, in that book, who arrived in Oxford, and all the undergraduates fell in love with her and ended up by throwing themselves in the river.'

'Zuleika Dobson,' said Vikki.

'That's the one.' Anna sighed. 'How can I compete, if Bruce should fall for her?'

'Beauty,' said Vikki, 'is more than skin-deep. And furthermore, is in the eye of the beholder.'

'And that,' Anna snorted, 'is a right load of cobblers if ever I heard one.'

## Third Week: Monday

Graham and Leonie were the last to arrive. 'This is Leonie Mitchell,' Graham said proudly, as though he, personally, were responsible for her creation.

'Hello, everybody.' Leonie smiled.

'Hello, Leonie.' Ben came striding down the hall to meet her. 'How lovely to see you. These are Vikki Maitland, Anna Freed, Ronny Benson, Peter Tilsley, Bruce Fontaine, Jack Muir and Sam Wolff.

51

Mike Ramsden who's doing the set, and Maddy Cameron who's in charge of wardrobe.'

'He's acting as if it's a bloody sherry party,' muttered Anna.

'She's dressed as though she thinks it is, too,' Vikki whispered back. 'Red leather trousers, whatever next?'

'This,' said Jack 'will put the cat among the proverbials. Ben is smitten.'

'Bruce looks as if he's about to faint,' Sam chortled. 'I think I might faint too. Does one ask such a treasure to a pizza lunch at the Fantasia? I hardly think so. Still, nothing ventured, etc.' He went over to where Leonie was standing.

'Beloved Leonie,' he bowed to her. 'We have only just met, but I feel that I have known you forever. Will you spend the next eternity with me, starting with a spicy Indian lunch at the Dildunia?'

'Is he always like this?' Leonie giggled and turned to Ben.

'Take no notice, Leonie. He is given to such flights of fancy. Sam, we're going to start work now. I want a good workout for everyone. Shake you all loose and get you going. Oliver, give us some heartwarming music on the piano, please.'

Music pounding in the high-ceilinged room. Stretching, bending, leaping, shaking. Maddy sits on the floor with Mike. She thinks: he has to be nice to her. She's new. We all know each other. It must be strange for her. All the men are showing off. I won't be jealous. I absolutely refuse.

'She'll be more trouble than she's worth,' said Mike.

'I think she's gorgeous,' Maddy answered.

'They'll all come and see the show, just to look at her. We must get her photo into *Cherwell*.'

Mike was gloomy. 'She'll be all over the front page before you can say "pizazz". Oh well, it's no skin off my nose.'

'Don't you like her, Mike?'

'She's O.K.' Mike grunted. 'Not exactly my type.'


## Wednesday

'Right, Leonie,' said Ben. 'From the top. You're a cellist, very proper and demure. The tune is fake Schubert, but you have to smoulder. Banked fires of passion, just waiting to break out, O.K.? What you're singing is going to be a contrast with how you look, see? That's where the joke is. Let's try it.'

Leonie sang, not terribly well.

'Marvellous,' said Ben, when she had finished. Vikki said: 'Wasn't that my song? Ben? Come on, concentrate!' Ben looked at her with the eyes of someone just coming out of a dream.

'Well, love. Don't worry, we'll find you another sketch or something. What about that school teacher one? Or the artist's model?'

'But this is my big number, Ben. You simply can't.'

'Vikki...' Ben took her aside. 'We must think of the show, mustn't we? Leonie just looks the part. I think I'll also team her with Bruce for the duet.'

'Anna will be delighted,' said Vikki, rage making her voice wobble. 'I'll tell you something, Ben

Ashworth. I'm not in the habit of letting people down, so I can't walk out at this stage, but I shan't be doing another show with you, not ever.' Vikki sat down, shaking.

'Oh Vikki, don't be so temperamental. You know we simply couldn't do without you.'

'You'll bloody well have to, when this lot's over, won't you?' Vikki turned away.

'Right, Leonie darling,' said Ben. 'Let's try it again.'

*Darling*, Maddy thinks. He doesn't mean anything by it. He's being theatrical. She spends the next few moments trying to remember if Ben has ever called Anna or Vikki darling. She is almost sure he hasn't.

## Fourth Week: Conversations during rehearsals

*Anna*: Leonie's going to the Elizabeth tonight. I heard her telling Jack.

*Vikki*: I hope she chokes on her crème brûlée.

*Maddy*: Who's she's going with? Did you hear?

*Anna*: Oh, no, shrouded in mystery. Someone rich, I imagine. Not one of us.

*Oliver* (whispering): Leonie – what about lunch tomorrow?

*Leonie*: Oh, Olly, I'd adore to, but I'm driving up to the Trout...

*Oliver*: Who with?

*Leonie* (emitting silvery laughter): He's rather a

bore, actually, but his car's such a pretty colour, I can't resist.

*Ben*: Does anyone know where Leonie is?

*Leonie* (arriving breathless at that moment): Sorry I'm late, everyone. I've just this minute stepped off the train from London. Frightfully dreary party, really. Will I be O.K. in this? (opening the front of her coat to reveal silk jersey clinging desperately to every one of her curves.)

*Ben*: Terrific, darling. You look divine.

*Leonie*: I feel like death warmed up. Could I have a coffee, someone?

*Graham*: I'll get you one at once.

*Anna* (sotto voce): What did your last servant die of?

## Fifth Week: Monday

In Ben's room in Paradise Square, Ben and Maddy were drinking coffee.

'I think,' said Ben, 'that they're all being most unreasonable. Leonie is ... physically right, that's all. It's nothing personal.'

'I know,' Maddy said, 'but you have edged Anna and Vikki practically out of the show. Two of Anna's songs to her, one of Vikki's and you've replaced Vikki in three sketches ...'

'They're being petty,' Ben said. 'Childish. Not troupers, any of them. It's the show that counts after all.'

'But she's not very good.'

'She's O.K. She'll be sensational. Wait and see. I know.'

'Fine,' said Maddy, standing up. 'Listen, I can't discuss it now. I've really got to fly, Ben.'

'Really? Can't you stay? It's only six.'

'No, I mustn't. Not tonight. I'm so behind with my work... no, Ben, don't... I can't, please...'

He was kissing her, ruffling her hair.

'O.K. kid. See you tomorrow at rehearsal then.'

'Bye,' said Maddy, and ran downstairs, waving.


One of these days, she thinks, it'll just slip out of my mouth. 'I love you', just like that. What will Ben say? Does he love me? Doesn't he? It feels as though he does when he kisses me, but why doesn't he say anything? Do men ever say it? I must ask Anna tomorrow.


Ben took the coffee cups into the tiny kitchenette.

'I've got you,' he sang, 'under my skin...'

A knock at the door. Probably Maddy back again. Maybe she's forgotten something, Ben thought as he went to the door.

'Hello, Ben.' Husky, vibrant. Leonie's voice. Leonie, in Paradise Square.

'Leonie, darling, how lovely to see you.'

'Can I come in for a minute?'

'Of course.' Ben held the door open.

She brushed past him as she came in. A fragrance drifted from her hair. 'Which is your room?'

'This one... it's a bit of a mess, I'm afraid.'

'It's lovely. May I sit here?'

'Yes, of course.'

'Come and sit next to me.' She looked up at Ben and smoothed the sofa cushion beside her. 'I really have to talk to you.'

Ben sat down rather gingerly, not too close. Leonie turned her face to him. Two pearly tears were making a rather elegant progress down her cheeks.

'I don't know what to do, Ben. They hate me so much. Vikki and Anna – maybe Maddy too. I do try to be nice to everyone, really I do, and I can't help it if Pete stares at me all the time, or if Sam takes me to lunch. Or if you give me all those things to do in the show. It's not my fault. Please, Ben, please make them see it's not my fault.'

Tears were dropping more swiftly now.

'Leonie – please don't cry. It'll be all right, you'll see.' Ben touched her hair tentatively, lifted her face and wiped away her tears with a rather grey handkerchief.

Later, going over what had happened, it all reminded him of something from a cheap romance. 'With one bound he leaped to her side and took her in his arms' etc., etc. No bounding had been necessary, of course. Weren't they both on the sofa? More of a slither and a twist, and there she was, and Ben had felt himself enfolded in long, smooth arms, and oh my God, legs too, and mouth and hair. For a split second, like a man drowning, he had grasped at the thought of Maddy. Then there were those lips again, brushing the lobe of his ear, burning on his neck and his mouth, and those hands were everywhere. Joyfully, he had plunged back into the sweet-smelling waves of feelings that had washed every other thought away.

## Tuesday: Monologue

*Ben to Maddy*: 'I can't help it, Maddy. You've got to see that. It's something... I don't know. Elementary, basic. It's, well, I know it sounds trite but it's bigger than both of us and I'm sorry. Maddy, please love. Don't look like that. I did want... I do... I mean, you're very important to me. I care about you. None of this means I don't care about you, 'cos I do. Honestly, if you could only understand what it feels like. Like being drunk all the time or drugged. I can't bear to be without her, I just want to – Maddy, where are you going? Maddy, come back, you haven't even finished your coffee. Maddy, listen, please...'

## Saturday: Monologue

*Anna to Vikki*: 'It was only the one night, honestly. Well I heard it from Bruce who heard it from Oliver, and he should know. Oliver says she's dangling Ben on a string, just when Ben thought he'd got it made. She won't even give him the dubious pleasure of her company at lunch in the Kings Arms, let alone anything else. Just bats her eyelashes and smiles, and he hangs about waiting for more. While off she slides with her grey little whoever-he-is in the cherry-coloured Jaguar at every opportunity. Ben looks half dead, though, doesn't he? That'll be Passion gnawing at his vitals, I daresay, and if ever vitals deserved to be gnawed, his do.'


## Sixth Week: Monday

Maddy is ironing clothes, ready for the dress rehearsal. She is pale. She is angry. She wishes she could scorch a huge great hole in Leonie's gold lamé trousers. She still loves Ben. It isn't his fault. He is bewitched. He has wandered through the last few days of rehearsal caressing Leonie with his eyes, sitting beside her during other people's numbers. He has been concentrating on her, thought Maddy, nothing else. The show will probably suffer. I don't give a damn. I don't care if it's a Summer Salad or a bloody Spotty Dick with lumpy custard.

'Maddy,' Ben bursts into the room. 'Where's Leonie?'

Maddy bites back all kinds of answers, such as 'In Hell, for all I care' and 'You should know' and says quietly: 'In her dressing-room, I expect.'

'But she isn't. I've tried. She's not in the other dressing rooms, either – or the Green Room.'

'Try the loo.' Maddy smiles.

'I have. She's not in the theatre. Maddy, what are we going to do? I called the half ages ago. What if she doesn't come? Oh God, it'll be a disaster.'

'I'm sure she will come,' said Maddy. 'She's very often late, you know.'

'But ... what if she doesn't?'

Maddy unplugged the iron. 'Anna and Vikki will share her numbers. They know them backwards.' It is a measure of how much I still love him, she thinks, that I don't point out to him that they were Anna's and Vikki's numbers in the first place.

A voice comes over the Tannoy: 'Quarter of an hour, please. Quarter of an hour.'

Maddy, her arms full of ironed dress shirts and frilly blouses, says, as she leaves for the dressing rooms: 'The show, as they say, must go on. What's happened to your pizazz, then?'

Ben moans.


## Tuesday

They had pushed together two tables at the Kemp. Sam was hiding something behind his back, and grinning. 'Where's Ben? Still pounding the pavements of Walton Street?'

'He'll be in later,' said Graham. 'What are you hiding?'

'Hiding? You must be joking. There's no hiding this. It's all over every breakfast table in the country. Only a small item in a gossip column, but still' – he flourishes a copy of the *Daily Express* – 'Listen:

"What will the venerable dons at one of our oldest institutions of learning think this morning when they discover that the Hon. Angus Potterton-Shrumley is absenting himself from tutorials? This column has it from an impeccable source that the

60

famous cherry-red Jaguar is at this very moment eating up the miles between Oxford and Gretna Green. The Hon. Angus is accompanied by none other than Leonie Mitchell, goddess of the London clubs." Sam looked up. 'Etc., etc and so forth. What do you all think of that?' They looked at each other, smiling.

'Frightfully unprofessional,' said Pete. 'Eloping just before a first night. I call it letting the side down.'

'Someone,' said Anna, looking directly at Maddy, 'had better break the news to Ben, and as for the rest of us, I propose we all have another round of tea cakes, just to celebrate.'

There is something special about first nights. Cards and telegrams are stuck into mirrors, flowers are pushed into old jam jars and grease paint really does smell of transformation and magic: a sweet fragrance. There are sounds, murmurings from the auditorium. Real people. A real audience. Lighting cues are checked, props are checked.

'Five minutes, please. Five minutes.'

Maddy is zipping Vikki into black crepe. Vikki has taken on a strangeness with her new beauty. Grey lines are sketched around her eyes, green eyeshadow glitters on her eyelids. Her mouth is painted crimson. Vikki catches Maddy's stare in the mirror and makes a face, makes fangs of her teeth.

'Ze Bride of Dracula rides again,' she says. Ben's

voice comes over the Tannoy: 'Hello, everyone. You'll be going on in a couple of minutes, so I'd just like to wish you all the very best of luck, and to say . . .' – a long pause – 'to say I'm sorry for the way I've been behaving lately. The way I've treated some of you. It was unforgiveable, and I don't deserve the fantastic performance that Vikki and Anna put on at such short notice. I'm O.K. now, though, and I hope . . . well, I know you'll slay 'em. Thank you.'

Maddy says nothing. Vikki winks at her in the mirror. 'I'd say,' she smiles, 'that that was your cue. I should go right down there to the prompt corner, and hoist him with his own pizazz.'

'Beginners, please,' says the Tannoy.

'Oh my God, am I O.K.? The hair – is it going to stay up? Oh, Maddy, I shall faint.'

'Nonsense,' says Maddy, pushing Vikki firmly out of the door. 'You'll knock 'em for six.'


Maddy can hear the opening music as she tidies up: throws away tissues and cotton wool, arranges Vikki's things on a chair. She can imagine, a little, the way they feel now, behind the footlights. Blue and pink and apricot squares of light shining up at them, changing them. This room is tidy, she thinks. There is nothing to stop me watching from the wings. She closes the dressing-room door behind her, and walks carefully downstairs towards distant noises of laughter and applause.


After the interval, Ben stayed behind in the Green Room with Maddy.

'I'll help you wash those cups,' he said. 'It's something to do. D'you think it's going O.K.? Oh, well, it's out of my hands now. Didn't you think Anna was marvellous in the Spanish number? I wish...'

'Ben,' said Maddy 'sit down and shut up and relax, for Heaven's sake. It's fantastic. It's marvellous. It'll get the best notices you've ever seen. People will flock. Now hush. Nip into the Gloucester Arms for a brandy if you like.'

'No, I'll sit here.' Ben sat on the lumpy armchair. Maddy washed cups. Neither of them said anything. At last, Ben stood up. He came and stood beside Maddy at the sink. 'Maddy?' he whispered.

'What?'

'Are we ever... I mean, do you think you could... Oh Lord, I'm making a pig's ear of this. Maddy, is it O.K.? For us? I'm sorry, you know, and I do miss you...'

Maddy looked at him. 'You've got a bloody nerve,' she said gently, drying her hands. 'But what can I do? I love you.' There, it's out, she thought, and blushed all over. I said it. He's looking as if he can't believe it. Why are men so stupid? Didn't he realize? What did he think?

'I didn't realize.' Ben was saying. 'Oh Maddy, I thought...'

'You're a fool,' said Maddy. 'Come on, let's go and watch the rest of the show.' She held out her hand and he took it.


'That's the fourth curtain-call,' said Maddy. 'And they want more.'

Ben turned to her. 'Oh, Maddy, listen to them! They love it, they really do.'

'I told you they would, didn't I?'

'Yes, you did. You told me a lot of things. Maddy?'

'Yes?'

'Leonie ... she was – a kind of virus. I mean, I've got over her, I really have.'

'I don't want to talk about Leonie.'

'I don't either.'

'Then why are we.'

'I don't know.'

'Ben?'

'Yes?'

'Will you please shut up and kiss me?'


The clapping that greeted the encore was deafening, but neither Maddy nor Ben heard it at all.

# PLAIN MISS

Miss van der Leyden was Under Matron and the girls had no nickname for her. Celia, prefect in charge of Terracotta Dormitory, tried calling her 'V.D.L.' for a while, but it never caught on. Miss van der Leyden was Under Matron and she was foreign. She came from Belgium.

*(What do you really know about Belgium? Anything? It's the top unknown country in the world. Hasn't got an image, you see, like Spain... bulls... castanets... frilly skirts... men in flat hats à la various advertisements for booze... Perhaps the whole country should get hold of a bloody good advertising agency. Belgium – O.K. try. Ypres, Flanders Fields, waffles, lace, linen, and flax and beetroot, and isn't there coal mining near the German border? Now, of course, it means the Common Market, but then it was faceless, stuck between France and Holland.)*

Miss van der Leyden was second-in-command to Mack, or Mighty Mack. The thin, greying and brittle-looking Miss McLaren of that ilk, who came from Scotland.

*(Scotland, unlike Belgium is a country with a very clear idea of what it is: hoots the noo, haggis, tartan and lang may your lumreek Jimmy.)*

Mighty Mack was very visible and very audible.

You could hear her coming. Her fluorescent voice echoed through Violet and Rose Dorms on sheet-changing day, floating ahead of her to the denizens of Terracotta in the satisfyingly rhythmic exhortation that had about it a whiff of the nautical, some of the splendour of the old clipper ships: 'Top to bottom and bottom away!'. That was the cry, time after time as they folded the bottom sheet and put it by the door of their cubicle (bottom away) ready for Laundry Collection, as they folded the hospital corners of the erstwhile top sheet under the mattress (top to bottom) and shook out the stiff, white expanse of the new top sheet, the girls all fully expected to hear 'Hoist the mizzen mask' or some such piratical command come flying through the air.

Mighty Mack strode through the dorms with never a backward glance. Miss van der Leyden limped behind her, gathering up the dirty bottom sheets and pushing them into a vast sack. As Mighty Mack left each dormitory it was Miss van der Leyden who hovered uncertainly in the doorway and reminded the girls of less pleasant things: knickers that needed changing, (Mon. Wed. Fri.), baths that had been inadequately cleaned, counterpanes left crooked. She did the dirty work.

As well as being foreign Miss van der Leyden was ugly. Neither plain, nor homely, nor ordinary, nor even unattractive, just ugly. This ugliness made her a constant source of interest to the girls. Such features were unusual. Did they betoken evil of some kind? Could she be a witch? A German spy? (Germany, Belgium, all foreign, all the same really, aren't they? Not much difference.) What was she doing here? How old was she? Was there something wrong with her leg, or did she just pretend to limp? After lights out on long, summer evenings when sleep was impossible, Terracotta Dormitory pondered the possibilities.

'I think,' said Celia (firm and sensible but with a soppy streak), 'that she's the youngest daughter of an aristocratic family. They're all ashamed of her, so they've sent her over here.'

'She ran away from home,' said Alison (a weed if ever there was one) 'because she had a cruel father who hated her because she was so ugly.'

'I think she's an ex-Nazi,' said Hazel. (Her taste ran to war books.)

'I think,' said Louise (Matron's pet on account of general daintiness and docility), 'that she's really a Princess only bewitched or something. I don't think anyone could be so ugly all on their own. They'd have to be bewitched.'

*(In the gym, Louise's feet are long and slim in black pumps. The bones of her ankles twinkle like jewels. Miss van der Leyden's ankle bones are drowned in flesh that slops over the edges of her lace-up shoes. The legs are encased in mud-brown lisle. One leg is a little shorter than the other.)*

Myra says nothing during these conversations. She is on Miss van der Leyden's side. It would never do to tell the others. Myra and Miss van der Leyden have a lot in common, Myra feels. They are both far from home. Myra has ceased to be homesick now, but she has not yet found roots here. She thinks of herself as an exile. Where she came from the sun shone, the sea was green glass, and flowers, trees, mountains, birds: everything was brightly coloured.

'Aren't you British?' the other girls had asked at first, ready to pounce, ready to reject her just on that account.

'Of course I'm British,' Myra answered. 'I come from a British Colony, after all.'

*(Well, all right. Colony. That's a word we know. You'll pass. Just. Not quite the Britishest British you can be. Not home Counties ponies in the paddock scones for tea British. But still, something.)*

Myra, as the others talk, thinks about the Michaelmas Term. Miss van der Leyden comes into her own in the Michaelmas term. Knitting is considered to be a suitable early evening occupation for the younger girls, and Miss van der Leyden is a knitter. Patiently, in still broken English she helps to cast on, she shows, she explains, she unpicks. She reworks all kinds of grubbly little efforts that have failed, and she says: 'Keep your work clean, look, like mine, no? Take care. Wash your hands before you knit...' Miss van der Leyden keeps her work in a white cloth edged with lace. Sometimes she takes it out to show the children and then oh, how their faces shine. How their mouths hang open, for here it is. Here is all the loveliness of leaves and twists. Tiny stitches, even beads and pearls knitted into the gossamer fabric: this is the beauty that Miss van der Leyden spins from the ends of her thick misshapen fingers, and the girls admire it, love it, envy it and forgive

70

Miss van der Leyden everything for the time being.

'It's lovely,' Myra said. 'Who is it for?'

'A shawl,' Miss van der Leyden answered. 'For my niece.'

'Does she live in Belgium?'

'Yes. In a house with a sloping roof. Near a canal.'

'Don't they have canals in Holland?' Myra asked.

'And Belgium.'

'Is your niece pretty?'

'Very pretty.' Miss van der Leyden smiled. 'The same as I am not pretty, so is she pretty. This shawl, it will be for a wedding, I think.'

Myra said nothing more, but looked at the shawl and imagined the niece with it round her shoulders, walking in a wedding dress beside a canal. Blue all around: blue sky curving above her from horizon to horizon like the inside of a porcelain bowl.


Years pass. Myra, Celia, Alison and the others grow too old to discuss Miss van der Leyden. They hardly ever think of her. She has become part of the school for them, and do you ever talk about your desk? Or the curtains in the school Hall? It is only when Miss Roach announces at end of term assembly that Miss van der Leyden is leaving 'after ten years of devoted service to the girls in her care,' that their curiosity is stirred. Myra even goes to say goodbye. She, of all of them, has not forgotten evenings in the Junior Common Room. She still remembers the dull green jumper with lace panel

71

across the front, which she never finished.

Miss van der Leyden is spooning Virol into an undersized new girl. 'I've come to say goodbye,' says Myra. 'I'm sorry you're leaving.'

'I, too, will miss you all,' Miss van der Leyden says. 'But it will be good to be at home at last...'

Myra has changed a little. She now feels that this is her home. The landscapes of her early childhood have become dim and faded, misty with neglect.

Miss van der Leyden smiles at Myra and winks. 'You remember the shawl? With the pearls? For a wedding?'

'Yes, of course,' Myra smiles. 'Did your niece like it?'

'Is for me,' Miss van der Leyden says triumphantly. 'For my wedding.'

Myra tries not to let her mouth hang open in amazement. She does not have to speak because Miss van der Leyden is talking, talking, talking... telling everything.


When Myra recounts the story to the others later, they don't believe it. Celia says:

'She was pulling your leg. I mean, it's strange enough to think of her getting married at all, but all that stuff about a love affair, and all those letters backwards and forwards all these years, and having to wait for his wife to die. And now his wife conveniently dying so they're going to live happily ever after... I just don't believe it. It's like those silly books that Louise goes in for. It's not like the kind of thing that happens to people like her.'

But Myra believes it. Why ever should Miss van der Leyden have lied to her? Now, she would think of the Under Matron as a symbol of hope and the possibility of finding happiness, and picture her in the gossamer shawl starred with pearls. Beside the canal. Blue curving over her head like the inner surface of a bowl.

# WE'LL MEET AGAIN...

'Fan-bloomin'-tastic!' Maddy said, as she peered short-sightedly into a mirror that was, as she put it, 'more spots than silver.'

She was wearing a brown felt hat and a brown woollen coat, with a fitted waist and a skirt that nearly touched the ground. 'This'll be more your size, Celia. You'd better try it on.' She took the coat off.

'Wherever did you get all this stuff? It's really amazing. I mean, it looks authentic.'

'It is authentic.' Celia was pulling the brown coat on.

'Honestly, Maddy, can't you do something about the mirrors? It's difficult to see what you look like. What kind of shop is this anyway?'

'It's not a shop. Hadn't you noticed? Just an oversized box full of second-hand clothes. My customers are used to it. If they want mirrors, they can go to Jaeger or Next or somewhere. Cheapo style, that's what I'm about. These are great, honestly. Forties is all the rage. You said they were authentic. Where did you find them?'

'I was given them. A man in our street let me take them. He was clearing up after his wife died.' Celia paused. 'She died about two years ago, actually. I think he couldn't bring himself to clear up her stuff, and get rid of it – not for ages. Anyway, when I got there, it was all ready in that box.'

'Dead sad, really,' said Maddy 'when you think of it. Did you know her? The wife?'

'Well,' said Celia 'by sight, you know. Not to talk to, not properly. My mum used to go in there and have a chat, now and then. She was fat. Not very pretty. Not when I knew her...'

Maddy had stopped listening and gone to lure a couple of helpless-looking people into her clothes-box. Celia stood in front of the mirror and tried to see herself in what little light there was. I look good, she thought. It suits me. Mrs. Stockton was skinny like me, back in the Forties. He said so. I wonder how much Maddy'll want for it.

Mr. Stockton was standing by the sideboard when I went in. 'Just a few things belonging to Irene,' he said, and twisted his head round as if he didn't want to look at anything. Not at me and not at the clothes. 'They're no good to me now.' That's what he said and then he laughed. Not much to Irene either for a long time. She got too big for them in the end.

'There was a time,' (he rubbed a clenched fist along the edge of his chin) 'when I could have put both my hands in a circle round her waist. She wasn't any thicker than you are now. A slip of a thing, was my Irene.' His throat filled up then, like someone with a chesty cough. I think he was having a hard time keeping himself from bursting into tears.

I said quickly: 'My friend Maddy'll like these. She's got a kind of stall in Affleck's Palace.' He didn't know about the Palace. I told him, 'it's where you go in Manchester for good, exciting

second-hand stuff. Is it all right?' I asked, 'Taking it
there . . .' He nodded then.

Yes, Irene was fond of young people, would like
to think of them enjoying her clothes. 'You should
try some,' he said, 'you're the right size.'

'Oh, I couldn't,' I said and now here I am in
Irene's coat, and he was right. It's beautiful. Anyway, then I couldn't think of anything else to say, so
I picked up the box. Looking back, I could see him
standing in the window, stroking the back of his
hand along his jawline.

'That looks great,' said Maddy, when the customers
had gone. 'You should keep it.'

'How much do you want for it?'

'I'll let you have it for nothing. A kind of
commission for bringing this treasure to me, and
not trying to flog it to anyone else. You can also
have a dress – there's got to be something . . .'

She started rummaging about in the cardboard
box. 'Here you go.'

She held out a soft, slippery bit of what looked
like nothing very much. 'Try that on.'

Celia went into the small space behind the bit-of-
fabric-on-a-string that served Maddy as a fitting
room. This isn't like me, she thought. These aren't
my type of clothes at all. Almost as though she had
overheard Celia's thoughts, Maddy spoke from
behind the curtain.

'I know it's not your type of gear, Celia. Not
really, but you should think about it seriously. I
mean, that Forties look really does something for
you. You can wear that dress to the Forties Night
next month.'

'What Forties Night?' Celia said, pulling the curtain back.

'Wowee!' Maddy shrieked 'you look like a film star from one of those old black and white thingies. What do you mean, "what Forties Night"? Every few months they have one, down at the Ritz. Everyone dresses up and the music is Glenn Miller and stuff like that. It's great – you must come, Celia. Promise you'll come.'

'Not got anyone to come with, have I?' Celia said, pulling the curtain across again. 'Still, I like the dress. I'll have that, and thanks a lot.'

'Don't mention it,' said Maddy. 'And you don't need to have a partner. You can come with me and Graham.'

Celia muttered something about gooseberries as the dress came up over her head.

'You'll meet someone there,' Maddy said. 'Do say you'll come. Go on – you've got such a perfect outfit, that dress in this wonderful slippery material with those lovely blue leafy patterns all over it. And the coat on top of course. Please, Celia?'

'Right,' said Celia. 'I'll come. I'll probably regret it, but I'll come.'

'Terrific,' said Maddy. 'Just for that, I'll let you take your things home in a carrier bag. It's not every customer who gets one of those. I can tell you!'

Later that same day, Celia struggled up the sloping pavement to the station, wishing the books she had to carry to college were lighter. Wishing that

Maddy's carrier bag had a decent handle, one that didn't cut your fingers as you held it. She was wearing the brown woollen coat, and had put her own anorak into the bag, but it didn't make it much lighter. She stood on the platform, waiting for the train to Birchwood, watching the dusk wrap itself, mauve and grey and pink, around buildings which suddenly looked soft at the edges. Only October, she thought, and the evenings are coming earlier and earlier.

When the train pulled in, she opened one of the doors, and then stood aside to let a weary-looking woman hung about with folding pushchair, crying baby and assorted bits of shopping, get on before her. As she slammed the door shut, Celia looked out of the window and the train slowly slid away from the station. Someone was standing on the platform, waiting, looking all up and down the line, as if expecting to see someone... Celia wasn't looking carefully, only caught a glimpse, and by the time she looked back to see, the figure had shrunk to almost nothing, but it seemed to her that the woman was wearing a brown coat very like hers. She was still peering up and down the platform, up and down... Oh well, Celia said to herself, Maddy said Forties styles were in. They're more in than she thought. I'd better find somewhere to sit.

Celia sat down in the first seat she could find. It wasn't a non-smoking compartment, but what the hell, only a ten-minute journey. I'm exhausted, Celia thought. She closed her eyes for a moment, thinking about the silky dress, dazzled for a second by a daydream of herself wearing it under one of those glass balls they had in dance halls, the kind that bounced darts of coloured light around the walls and on to the skin and hair of all the dancers. She opened her eyes.

'Do you mind if I smoke?' said the young man who was now sitting opposite her.

'No . . . not at all,' Celia said. Where on earth had he come from? How long, she wondered, have I been sitting here with my eyes closed? She glanced down at her watch . . . only a minute or so. He must have slipped in quietly. He's very polite. Fancy asking if I minded him smoking.

Celia looked at him as he turned his head to look out of the window. Some kind of a soldier, some sort of uniform. Very fair hair. Dyed? thought Celia. You never knew, nowadays. But dark eyes – maybe blue, but dark. A parting in the hair, short at the back and sides and floppy at the front. As the train came into Birchwood, the young soldier stood up smiled at Celia.

'Cheerio,' he said, and turned and walked down the compartment towards the door.

''Bye,' said Celia, still a little faint from the feelings brought on by that smile. I can't run after him, she thought. I'll use the other door. She jumped on to the platform and looked for him. There he was, already over the bridge and on the other side. I should go after him, she thought. Call out to him . . . being dignified and ladylike doesn't matter anymore – what if I never see him again?

'Stop it!' Celia said aloud to herself and she turned round to make sure she was alone. As she trudged over the bridge to where her father was waiting for her in the car, she told herself over and over again that she had only seen him for a few moments, that she would probably never see him again. And that she was being a fool. Nevertheless, she knew what it felt like to fall in love. It was as unmistakeable as getting a cold, and she recognized within herself all the symptoms: the pain she felt at the very idea of never seeing him again made her want to cry. The headlights of her parents' car broke into a thousand small fragments of light in the tears she hadn't quite managed to blink away.

'I saw you on the train the other day, didn't I?'

'Yes, you asked if you could smoke,' Celia said. (Oh, Glory be, here he is again... ten whole minutes... please, God, let the time go slowly... slow it up... let him like me... thank goodness I'm wearing the brown coat.)

'Well,' said the soldier 'it's only polite to ask. I should introduce myself. My name's Neville.'

'Mine's Celia.'

'Delighted to meet you.'

(What a funny way he has of talking, Celia thought. None has ever said that to me. *Delighted to meet you...*)

'Do you live in Birchwood?'

'I do at the moment, of course,' Neville said. 'Based there, you know. Training.'

'Training for what?'

'Army, of course. Lots of chaps training up here, now.'

'Oh.' Celia was silent, racking her brains. She'd never seen any soldiers around Birchwood, she would certainly have noticed. But then, she'd only lived there a short time. Perhaps it was possible – maybe even a highly secret camp that no one was supposed to know about. Celia was bored by military matters and thought of a way to change the subject.

'Are you meeting someone in Manchester?' she asked.

'Yes, as a matter of fact. It's – well it's a young lady.' Neville blushed.

Celia stared at him. She hardly knew anyone who blushed like that. She sighed. That's that, she thought. He's got a girl friend. Wouldn't you know it? First time for six months I meet a decent bloke and someone else has got there first...

'Perhaps I'll see you again,' he said.

'Yeah,' Celia said. ''Bye.'

She muttered to herself as she walked towards the barrier: forget him. Forget him... he'll never be for you. He loves someone else. As she left the station she looked back towards the platform. Neville still there, waiting. Hope she never shows up, Celia thought. Hope she's run away to Brazil with a second-hand car dealer. Hope she never comes back. I'll take care of Neville.


Celia looked at the lines of rain slanting across the window. Was that the same young woman, still waiting for someone? She was standing on the platform, waiting, but it was hard to see, through all that rain, who it was. The train pulled out of the station.

'It's Celia, isn't it?' A voice interrupted her thoughts.

'Hello, Mr. Stockton. Fancy seeing you here.'

'It's a bit late for you, young lady, isn't it?'

'Not really. I often go home on this train after a film or something. Mum or Dad meet me. We'll give you a lift as well.'

'That'll be grand,' Mr. Stockton sighed. 'On a night like this.'

Celia said: 'Those clothes you gave me . . . . I hope you don't mind. I kept a coat and a dress.'

Mr. Stockton looked at Celia out of dark eyes.

'Mind, child? I'm delighted. Irene would have been delighted. She did think a lot of you. I know that. A properly brought-up child she said, not like some. And I'm glad someone young'll be wearing her things again. You look a little like her . . . she was thin. Had the same colour hair too. Fine, like a baby's it was, that soft. Eeh, I wish I had a pound for every time I've been up and down to Manchester on this line. I did my training up at Birchwood during the war, like many others, you know. Oh yes. And back and forwards I used to go, to meet Irene in Manchester.'

'Did you go dancing?'

Mr. Stockton chuckled. 'Yes, dancing, and to the cinema and did a bit of spooning too . . .' he sighed. 'Same as you get up to with your young man, I've no doubt.'

'I haven't got a young man,' Celia said.

'You will have,' Mr. Stockton said. 'There's no rush.' Celia opened her mouth to tell him about Neville, then changed her mind. She said nothing.

'Nearly home now,' said Mr. Stockton. 'There was a time when it was all aircraft noises round here. In the War.'

'You look – different, tonight,' said Neville. 'I mean you look very smart, of course, and you remind me...'

'Yes?' Celia asked.

'Well, you remind me of someone.'

'Is it your friend? The young lady you're always going to meet?' Celia was all dressed up for Forties Night at the Ritz in the silky dress and the brown woollen coat.

'Yes – yes you look very much like her. Especially now. Have I told you that before?'

'Once or twice.'

Neville looked away. 'I'm sorry. You see, it's not that I don't like you. I like you most awfully – I mean I *could* like you, but I have promised her...'

'But you say she's never there. Never at the station where she said she was going to be.' Celia's voice was full of anger. 'I hate to say this, but I think she's gone off you. I do really. Otherwise, why doesn't she turn up, eh? Honestly, Neville, face the facts. Please.'

The train was slowing down. The lights of the platform slipped past the window like bright beads. Celia stood up and Neville followed her.

'Celia!' Neville put out a hand, touched her sleeve.

'Yes?'

'You don't understand. I *have* to meet her – she's waiting for me, it's just that I have to find her... You can't possibly understand.'

'Don't talk about understanding,' Celia shouted. 'I'm fed up with it. Damn it, where's all your fine understanding? Can't you see that I love you? What do I have to do? Walk around with a sign on?'

Neville took Celia's face in his hands and kissed her softly on the mouth, so softly that she hardly felt it, and yet a shiver ran through her as if his lips had been ice-cold.

'I didn't know,' he said. 'I'm sorry. But I have to wait for her. I didn't know.'

The train stopped. Celia tore the door open, jumped out and ran towards the barrier. Through a fog of tears she could see Maddy.

'What's the rush?' Maddy said. 'You look as if you're running to save your life.'

'It's Neville. I'm fed up with him.'

'Ah, the mysterious unknown soldier. Let's get a squint at him. Where is he?'

'Up there, probably. That's where he usually is. Hanging about. Waiting for her.'

'Can't see a thing. Not a handsome soldier in sight anywhere. Come on, chuck, let's go and rustle up some grub, and then hit the Ritz with everything we've got.' Maddy shimmied down the hill towards Oxford Road singing, asking innocent passers-by whether this was, indeed, the Chattanooga Choo-Choo. Celia followed her, stiff with misery.

'It isn't that bad, is it?' asked Maddy.

'It's terrible. All those people sweating and everybody looking so – so –'

'So what?'

Celia sighed. 'So *fleshy*. So . . .' She could find no words.

Maddy put an arm around her shoulders. 'You

don't mean any of that. You mean, they weren't this Neville of yours.'

'He's not "of mine",' Celia said. 'He's someone else's. I'm sorry, Maddy, I'm going home. You and Graham stay. I'll be O.K. Station's only across the road. Can you phone my mum and tell her I'm on the 11.18? I don't feel like talking to her – and I can't stand the music, Maddy, and that's the truth.'

'What's the matter with it? It's great.'

'It makes me feel like crying. All that stuff about not knowing where and not knowing when, and the blue skies driving dark clouds far away. I've never really thought before, what it must have been like' – she paused – 'to be in love with someone who could die at any moment, and to be in danger yourself.'

'Go home,' said Maddy. 'I can see what kind of mood you're in. And Graham's walking you up the hill, and I don't care what you say.'

'I'll go and get my coat,' Celia said.


Celia huddled against one of the pillars, trying not to be seen. The clock on the platform said 11.15. Three more minutes... Oh, please, *please*, she thought, make him not look up. Make him not see me. She bit her lip and felt hope, any hope she had at all, drain out of every bit of her. Across on the other platform she could see them quite clearly, standing under one of the lights. They stood close together. He had found her at last, his girl, the one he had been coming to meet all those other times.

He was looking down at her. She seemed to fit herself into the circle of his arm, khaki against the brown fabric of her coat. A coat a lot like this, Celia thought, and glanced at them again. They had turned to leave now. Neville still had his arm around the woman. It seemed to Celia that his arm was fixed there forever, that nothing could move it. At the barrier they stopped and the woman stood on tiptoe so that he could kiss her. Celia watched them and felt sick. Where the hell was the train? She began to cry as it came into the station.

'Lovey,' said Celia's mother, 'what is it? What's happened? You surely can't have heard...'

'No, I'm fine... really. I just – it doesn't matter. Heard what?'

'About poor old Mr. Stockton.'

'What about him?'

'He died. Just about half an hour ago, that's all.'

'How do you know?'

'Betty told me. She heard a crash. He'd pulled an armchair over as he fell. It was very quick. He can't have felt any pain. Poor thing... I feel sad. He hasn't any children or close family that we know of. I'll have to go over there and help Betty pack up his stuff. Tomorrow probably, or the next day. D'you want to give me a hand, love?'

'Might as well,' said Celia. I don't think I'll ever care strongly about anything ever again, she thought. My whole body feels like a mouth does after an injection at the dentist's. Numb, but with layers of pain hidden away, hidden deep down and far away.

The darkness makes you silly, Celia thought the next day. She and her mother and Betty, Mr. Stockton's next door neighbour, were packing the old man's life away in cardboard boxes. Yesterday he was here, and now he isn't, she said to herself. Yesterday, when Neville kissed me in the corridor of the train, I thought there was a chance, a hope of something, and now I know there isn't. I should be able to pack the remains of what I feel into a box and give it to Oxfam. Get rid of it.

'How are you getting on?' Celia's mother shouted from the kitchen.

'Fine,' Celia yelled back. 'Just doing these albums...'

'Having a peep, are you?' Celia's mother came into the room.

'Can't help it. I'm nosey and I love all these old brown photos. Only some of them are so small, you can hardly see what anybody looks like.'

'There's one fallen out, Celia. Be careful.'

Celia's mother bent to pick up the photograph. She smiled. 'This is a bit more like it. A bit bigger. Goodness, look at Irene Stockton on her wedding day! During the War, it must have been – he's in uniform. Registry Office wedding, of course. Look how thin and pretty she was, and as for him, well, you'd never believe it was the same person as our Mr. Stockton. Here, take it and push it in somewhere. I've got to get back to the kitchen...' Celia's mother left the room.

Celia sat looking at the photograph for a long time, and allowed herself to cry. Not for Mr. Stockton, who had found his Irene at last, pretty in her silky, leaf-strewn dress and brown woollen coat. Nor for Neville, the young soldier Mr. Stockton used to be, whose face smiled up at her now from the wedding photograph. But for her own mixture of regret and happiness: regret because she knew that she would never see him again, and happiness in discovering that love was indeed, as she had always suspected, stronger than death.

# TWELVE HOURS –
## NARRATIVE AND PERSPECTIVES

## 3.30 p.m. Friday afternoon. Early July.

Linda Taylor, forty years old, locked the front door behind her and walked to the corner of Marlowe Avenue trying very hard to look as though she was merely slipping out to the shops. You never knew who might be watching. She'd said so to Alex, and told him to wait for her round the corner.

As soon as she was in the car, as soon as the door was shut, Alex's arms were around her. He was kissing her. She was breathless, laughing, trembling.

'Not here, Alex,' she said. 'Someone could see...'

'So what? I love you. I want you. I'm going to shout it out of this window –' he began to wind it down.

'Stop it, Alex! I haven't breathed a word to Beth.'

'She must have guessed. I'm practically a fixture in your house.'

'Well, she knows you're a friend, of course she does. But –' Linda hesitated ' – she doesn't know the full extent.'

'Don't be so sure,' Alex said, and began to drive away. 'These teenagers know all about it. Every detail. Innocence is a thing of the past, I'm told.'

'But I'm her mother,' Linda said, sighing. 'You

can imagine all kinds of things, but that's impossible . . . Can you imagine *your* mother . . .?'

Alex wrinkled his nose. 'The mind boggles.'

'Exactly.'

*When Beth was born, she lay in a perspex cot: you could look through and see her tiny hands like pink sea creatures, waving above the cellular blanket. I lay in bed and stared at her for hours. It wasn't only love washing over me, it was a kind of terror. I thought then: this is what always and forever mean. Every single thing she does from now until the moment of my death will be of the utmost importance to me. And it is. The most important thing.*

## 4.00 p.m.

Beth Taylor rang the front door bell. There was no answer. Wearily she lifted the school bag off her shoulder and rooted around in one of the pockets for the back door key and let herself in. This was not an unusual occurrence. Linda worked as a secretary in a school nearby and never knew if the Head was going to pop in at half past three and tell her to type out a rivetting letter about the spread of nits among the second year Juniors. Also, she sometimes had to shop on the way home. There was a note on the kitchen table.

'Dear Beth,

There's a meeting after school, today, and then Alex and I are going to a movie and dinner. Sorry

about this, but it only came up at lunchtime. Help
yourself out of the freezer for your supper and do
phone Pam or Rosie or Jean to visit you, but no
orgiastic teenage parties, please!

> See you later
> Love,
> Mum.'

Beth swore under her breath, screwed up the
note and threw it into a corner. Then she
telephoned Pam.

'Come over after you've had supper,' she said.
'I'm all on my own. My Mum's out gallivanting
again.'

'Right,' said Pam. 'See you about seven thirty.'

*Before the divorce, she was always there. That was the
main thing about her: her constant presence. There
always used to be a smell about the kitchen of cooking.
Cakes and ratatouille mixed in with her smell – a pale
pink, dusty sort of smell, like old roses. I know, I know,
said the poor distraught child, turning her tear-stained
face away from the TV cameras. A Broken Home how
sad, how awful, how will I ever grow up to be anything
other than a delinquent? But it wasn't like that. It was
what they call a 'civilised divorce'. Everyone is still
friends... or says they are. I still see my Dad...
nothing's really changed, because I never saw him much
anyway, he was always away / abroad / busy, and now
he's all those things still, only not in this house. The
divorce didn't make much difference to me, but it changed
Mum. She got a job, and she got a freezer. And now
bloody Alex, who's practically my age. Alex is O.K. I
suppose. She could have told me a bit earlier, though.*

*Prepared me. That's the trouble with grown-ups. No consideration for anyone else. Selfish.*


## 5.00 p.m.

'Last time I skyved off, I was twelve,' Linda said.

'What did you tell them?'

'That I was sick. That I'd be back O.K. on Monday.'

'And do you feel guilty?'

'Guilty as hell. But not on their account.'

Alex turned to look at her, and raised an eyebrow.

She said: 'It's Beth . . . how do you think she'd feel if she knew her mother'd been making love half the afternoon? It's naughty.'

'But nice. Like the cream cakes. Come here.' Linda moved into the curve of Alex's arm and closed her eyes.

*After Clive left, I thought I'd never feel anything again. Then Alex came to the school, and the very first time I saw him, I grew soft all over. For ages I just looked at him whenever I got the chance and wanted him like mad. I was like a kid, stupid and tongue-tied, rushing down certain corridors, going home down certain streets in the hope of bumping into him. I couldn't believe, still can hardly believe, that he felt what he said he felt. The first time he kissed me, behind the door of the stationery room, (what a cliché!), I blushed and nearly fainted, like a young girl, weak under his hands. Now when I'm with him, it's like being drunk. It's heat and light and I have no control over myself. I'm not behaving in a grown-up fashion. He's ten years younger than I am. His skin is smooth like a small child's. When I'm with him, he's all I can think about. I've tried to be discreet at school, but I feel like a Ready Brek advertisement, glowing all over, all the time.*

## 7.45 p.m.

'I think,' said Pam, 'that he's quite fanciable, from what I've seen.'

'He's all right, I suppose,' said Beth. 'If you like the doomed poet type: all floppy blonde hair and long fingers.'

'I wouldn't say no.'

'I would,' said Beth. 'I think there's altogether too much sex about. I don't reckon it's good for you.'

'Rubbish. Who said so?'

'I've read all about it.' Beth held up her hand and ticked the points off, one by one. 'First off, you can get pregnant. Then, if you go on the pill, your hormones get mucked about, then you can get herpes and stuff like that, and then they say you can get cancer of the cervix from it. Seems a bit bloody hazardous to me.'

'When you're in love,' Pam said 'you don't think about all that. You get carried away.'

'I call that,' Beth said, 'irresponsible. She's my mum. She's got no right to get carried away. She's got me to think of, hasn't she?'

'But she isn't fifteen, is she? All those things you mentioned are only supposed to happen to people our age, not to mums. Probably grown-up propaganda to stop us having fun.'

'I don't know about fun so much – it sounds a bit messy and revolting to me.'

'It's all different when you're in love,' Pam said firmly.

'But how on earth are you meant to know when you *are* in love?' Beth sighed.

Pam pondered this problem for a moment. 'You know you're in love,' she said firmly 'when all that stuff *doesn't* seem messy and revolting any more.' She looked at her watch. 'Isn't it time for that movie on telly?'

*She's changed, there's no doubt about that. Her clothes are different. Well, before she only ever stood about the house and did housework, or dug in the garden, so jeans and a baggy old sweater were O.K. Now she has to have decent clothes for school, I understand that, but I don't just mean her clothes. She's had her ears pierced, and wears long earrings that catch the light, and she's changed her perfume. It's not soft pink roses any more. It's a brown, smooth, thick smell, like fur. Perhaps Alex gave it to her. She wears blusher. I caught her putting on her makeup the other day. Her bra was pink and lacy and her bosom seemed to be slipping out over the top. Her knickers were like tiny little lace-trimmed shorts. I asked her about them and she said they were new and did I like them, but she was blushing like crazy, all the way down her neck, and she dressed very quickly after that. That was when I began to suspect about Alex. There's a couple writhing around on telly this very minute. If I think of Alex and Mum doing that, I feel quite ill. I wonder if Pam really likes this film. I wouldn't mind turning over to another channel.*

## 2.30 a.m.

Linda leapt out of bed.

'Alex! Alex, wake up, for heaven's sake! Look at the time – it'll be morning at this rate before I get home. Come on, Alex, please, wake up! Beth'll be worried frantic . . . please.'

Alex yawned and stretched and smiled.

'Relax. It's O.K. I'm awake now. I'll be ready in two shakes of a lamb's tail. And don't worry about Beth. She's a big girl. She'll have gone to sleep hours ago.'

'Please hurry, Alex.' Linda sighed. 'I knew we shouldn't have come back here for coffee after dinner. I knew at the time it was a mistake.'

'No, you didn't. You couldn't wait. Go on, admit it . . .'

'I admit it, I admit it. Now for the last time, will you get your shoes on, and let's get out of here!'

*I wish he could drive faster. I wish we could be home sooner. Oh, please, let Beth be O.K. Let her not be worried. Let the house not have burned to the ground, let there not be a mad axeman on the loose. Please, please, don't let me be punished. I know I shouldn't have gone back for coffee, but please let it be all right and I'll never do it again. It's just that every second since she was born*

101

*I've thought about every one of my actions in relation to her. Will Beth be O.K.? Want to go to the hairdresser? Then fix someone to pick her up from school. Want to go to the movies? Find a babysitter. Beth twenty minutes late back from school? All kinds of horrors flying behind the eyes. Now that she's a little older, nearly a grown-up, I feel as though I'm able to do certain things without looking over my shoulder to make sure she's all right. But not everything. Please, Beth, be all right. Don't be angry. Please understand.*

## 3.30 a.m.

'Mum, is that you?'

'Ssh. Yes, it's me. Are you O.K.?' Whispering.

'You don't need to whisper. I'm not asleep.'

Linda came into Beth's room and sat down on the bed.

'Haven't you been asleep at all?'

'Oh, yes, on and off. In between worrying myself sick about you . . . where the hell have you been? It's half past three in the morning.'

'Oh, Bethy, my love. I'm so sorry. I was having such a good time . . . I just forgot about the time – I'm really sorry. I won't do it again, I promise.'

'I thought you might have had a car crash . . . you could have rung up, couldn't you, when you knew you'd be late. Couldn't you? And what are you giggling about?'

Linda had started to laugh, and now, weak from lack of sleep and relief that Beth was there, just the same under her flower-printed sheets, her laughter grew and grew until the tears were streaming down her cheeks.

'You should hear yourself– you sound like a mother, you do honestly, and me... I feel like a juvenile delinquent.'

'Delinquent, yes. Juvenile – I'm not quite so sure...' Beth, happy to have her mother home again, even wearing new perfume, began to laugh as well.

*It's like one of those books where someone wakes up one day and she's turned into someone else. Or when a family discovers their child is really a mouse or something. There's a famous one where a guy wakes up and finds he's become this huge cockroach-type creature. You can see someone's point of view much better from another perspective. I always used to get dead irritated when I'd come home late and see Mum peering down the road, all white-faced and frowny, but I know how she feels now. She wasn't at the movies till 3.30. She must be sleeping with Alex. That'll take some getting used to. I must get used to it. I will.*

# SNAPSHOTS
# OF PARADISE

'You some kind of cousin or something, is that right?' Gene lay on his back on the grass and looked at Fran.

'I suppose I am,' she said. 'I don't think I know the proper name for it. My Great-grandmother and Grandma Sarah were sisters.'

'How come she cut and run all the way over there to England, then? Whyn't she stay here?'

Fran considered. Finally: 'She never said. But she never really became English, you know. Even after all the years. She still felt she belonged here.' Fran waved her hand to include not only the garden and the white frame house behind them, but the road and the apple orchard, the country, the state and the crazy quilting of all the other states. Coast to coast, mountain and river, shanty and skyscraper – her great-grandmother's beloved U.S. of A.

'Betcha nearly took a fit when you heard what she'd left you in her will,' Gene chuckled.

'She wasn't a rich woman,' Fran said. 'She didn't leave much. I think an airline ticket is a very good thing to leave someone.'

'You saying you couldn't have made it over here without her help?'

Being poor was not something Gene could easily imagine, Fran knew. She felt a desire to punch her newly-discovered cousin or whatever he was right

107

on his freckled nose. Spoilt brat! But:

'No, I couldn't,' she answered shortly. After all, she reminded herself, you are a guest in this house.

'Well, you sure picked yourself a fine time,' said Gene. 'Sixtieth wedding anniversary and all.' He nodded at the grown-ups clustering under a huge elm tree. 'I don't know why they have to get Ma Jenkins to take the photo. Family group, they call it, like it was something special. I could've done it.'

'But then you wouldn't have been in it.'

'What about Harry? What're they going to do about him?'

'Patti said they'd bring him down in his wheelchair . . .'

Gene rolled over on the grass, doubled up with laughter. 'Hey, that's terrific. That's just about going to kill Harry off, you know what I mean? Can't you just see it? A photograph on someone's table or something for ever and ever, and who's the one in a wheelchair? Grandpa, who's eighty-four? No? Then Grandma Sarah perhaps, who still looks like she could shimmy all night? Maybe Jo, or Patti, or one of the aunts? Maybe Jean, who's always looked half dead? Oh, no sirree, that there's Harry in the wheelchair . . . Remember him? Track champion? Cheerleaders' darling? Golden Boy? Superman of 1983 and all the years before that? Isn't that peachy? Just terrific. He's sure gonna love you for that, honey.'

'Me?' Fran said, 'Why me? I didn't have anything to do with the crash. That happened weeks ago, before I ever got here. Why should he blame me?'

'Won't blame you for the crash, kiddo. Blame

108

you for the snapshot.'

'But why? It wasn't even my idea, this family group. I think it was your mother...'

'But you're the cousin specially over here visiting all the way from England. Stands to reason you've got to have a shot of the family, right? Besides, it's your camera.'

Fran was silent. She glanced towards the house. Sure enough Eleanor, Gene and Harry's mother was pushing a wheelchair across the grass. Harry's hair fell over his brow, shadowing his eyes.

'Why did you call him a Golden Boy?' she asked Gene. 'His hair is dark. Almost black. You're more golden than he is.'

'Boy, are you dumb!' Gene sat up. 'Goldenness doesn't have one single thing to do with hair. Golden, that's the kind of person you are. Successful, handsome, smart. You get what I mean. It's up here.' He tapped his skull and laughed. 'I'm about as golden as a pair of sneakers with holes in them. Listen to it – you can't hear what they're saying, but I'll tell you: "Harry, how is it? How's it going, kid? Won't be long before you're back in training... Are you too hot? Too cold? Is everything o.k.? Would you like to sit here? Or over there, honey? Is the sun in your eyes? Move that wheelchair a little bit, Eleanor..." I could go on and on.'

'He's been injured,' said Fran. 'It's only natural that they should make a fuss over him. I think you're just plain jealous.'

'I guess,' Gene said. 'I guess I am. It's the natural condition for an Ugly Duckling born a brother to the swanniest swan of the lot.'

'And look what happened to the Ugly Duckling, Gene,' said Fran. 'Anyway, you're not one. Not really. Your nose is out of joint, that's all.'

'What does that mean? Boy, do I love your English expressions. Person can never tell what you're saying.'

'It means – I guess it means you're angry, jealous. I don't know.'

'Well,' Gene sighed. 'I should be used to it by now. I've lived with it for sixteen years. Ain't nothing new to me.'

Joe, Gene's grandfather, hurried towards them. From a distance, with his crew-cut hair and military style shirt, he looked like a young man.

'C'mon, you kids. Time to get lined up now.' Gene and Fran scrambled to their feet and walked over to where the others were in the process of sorting themselves out. Patti, Joe's wife and Gene and Harry's grandmother, seemed to be in charge of organizing the group.

'O.K. now. We've got Grandma Sarah and Grandpa right in the middle. Leave a space behind them for Joe and me, right? Then I guess . . . Yeah, Susan, Rose and Jean, can you kind of group yourselves around Grandma Sarah? Right, that's great. Where's that husband of your's, Rose? Oh! O.K. Bill, I've got you now. Whyn't you come over and stand by Grandpa? That's just fine. Eleanor, you still count as one of the younger generation. Come on down here now, near the front, and you kids, right in the bottom row. Let's put Franny between the boys, O.K. Kneel down, that's it. Cross-legged would be even better. Great. We've got it. Now don't move a muscle, anyone. I'll just race round to the back, then you can go ahead and press that button.'

Patti tottered across the grass in high-heeled sandals. Ma Jenkins, an unsuspecting neighbour who'd only called in on her way to church to wish the old folks a happy anniversary, came forward hesitantly.

'Lordy, what a responsibility! Is this right? Do I have to focus it? Is this the right button? Gee, I'll feel just terrible if it doesn't come out.'

She pressed the button. The photograph slid out of the bottom of the camera. The family group broke up and gathered round Ma Jenkins to watch the ghostly shapes sharpen, to watch the colours brighten.

'Just plain old magic, that's what it is,' said Ma Jenkins as she handed the camera back to Fran, relieved that her part in the adventure was over.

## 10.00 a.m. Family Group

*Grandma Sarah looks pretty in a lace blouse, not much different from the way she looked back in the 1920s when she used to Charleston all night in beaded dresses. She has been married for sixty years to the same man: Grandpa, who used to be a snappy dresser and now wears a beach shirt with palm trees printed on it. Patti has on a shirtwaister dress and wears her hair in bangs. She looks like an older version of Doris Day. The three weird sisters, (as Gene has liked to call them ever since he read 'Macbeth' in High School), don't look like sisters at all. Not to each other and not to upstanding, military Joe, who is their brother. Susan is the plump and homely one. She has harlequin glasses and a big smile. Rose is the skinny, glamorous one, gold bangles and*

111

*heavy rings weighing down her hands. Bill, her husband, is*
*half-hidden behind Joe. That's typical. Jean looks like an*
*old lady, although she's younger than all of them. It's the*
*hair in the bun, the brooch at the collar of the plain white*
*blouse. It's the eyes. Grandma Sarah has eyes with more*
*youth in them. Eleanor looks like a sister to her sons. Her*
*long, reddish hair falls over her face. Her skirt is pink*
*cotton, Mexican, embroidered with flowers and birds in fire*
*colours. Fran, Gene and Harry are at the front. Fran is*
*wearing jeans and T-shirt, looking quite American for a*
*beginner. Gene is looking at her. She is looking at Harry.*
*And Harry is looking straight at the camera.*


I suppose, Fran had thought when she first saw the
swimming-pool, that this is what they mean by
Culture Shock. A week of being in the United
States still hadn't accustomed her to the idea that
ordinary people (well, quite wealthy, O.K. but not
disgustingly, stinkingly rich) had such things right
in their back garden. She spent a lot of time there,
partly because she liked swimming, partly because
it was so hot and partly to talk to Harry. Mostly,
perhaps to talk to Harry. Ever since the crash, he
had made a kind of den for himself down by the
pool, under an umbrella, with a table next to him,
and all the comforts of his room around him, it
seemed. Gene had rigged up a portable T.V., he
had a radio, there were books – anything he could
possibly want. Fran felt newly shy each day as she
approached him. She felt she was invading his
privacy. And today? Would he be angry with her
about the photograph? He didn't look angry. He

was smiling.

'Hey, Fran,' he called as he saw her coming down the steps from the house. 'Come on over and talk to me. I'm going crazy in all this heat with no one to talk to...'

'Sure,' Fran said and sat down beside him. 'What do you want to talk about today?'

'I dunno. Life, Love, Art, Death, the usual stuff. You liking it here?'

'It's wonderful. I mean it.' Fran laughed. 'I never thought it'd be anything like this.'

'"Paradise for Kids" my grandmother calls it. Gene and me, we always call it that – I guess it was a kind of paradise when we were kids. But now, we say it kind of sarcastically, know what I mean? I mean the joint round here is not exactly jumping...'

'Do you miss the city? Is that it?'

'I guess – my friends, more than anything. And there's nothing to do except talk to your own family. That's why I like talking to you. You're different.'

Fran blushed. 'Different – is that good or bad?'

'It's good. I like it. I like hearing about England and the stuff you do back there. And I can tell you things. You're family and not family at the same time. D'you know what I mean?'

'May I ask you something then?' Fran said.

'Sure – anything you like.'

'Tell me about your father. No one ever mentions him.'

Harry frowned and said nothing for a moment. Fran looked at him: the smooth brown line of his neck, his straight nose, the toes sticking out of the

113

plaster casts he wore on both legs, and felt as though some part of her, some inner substance of which she was unaware, were dissolving, melting in the warmth of the love she was feeling. She identified it as love at that moment, while she was waiting for Harry to speak. She hadn't thought of it by a name before, only that she liked to look at him, liked the sound his voice made, waited for him to come into a room if he were absent, thought of him, imagined..

Now that she had given it a name, Fran felt both anguish and relief. Relief, because it's always a comfort to know the actual name of the disease you're suffering from, and anguish because in five days she would be back in England and Harry would be here, and that would be that. But, said a tiny, hopeful voice from somewhere inside her head, what if he loves you? Really loves you? He could visit... You could visit... You could marry, have kids. Paradise for kids. Live in Paradise...

Another voice, stronger, harder, so much more sensible, also inside her head: 'Don't be a bloody fool. Why should he love you? Look at you? Kiss you? Want to marry you, for Heaven's sake? Are you nuts? A face like that? A body like that? A Golden Boy? Forget it.'

Fran could picture Harry's future with a certainty that muffled her heart and made her catch her breath: Mr and Mrs Golden, right here in Paradise, a modern equivalent of Grandpa and Grandma Sarah. Almost, she could imagine Harry's sixtieth wedding anniversary... Forget it, she thought. Take it out at night, this love and look at it for a while before sleeping. Keep the 'what ifs'

114

and the 'maybes' for the dark hours. Don't let this love out into the open.

'Aren't you listening to me, Fran?' Harry said.

'Of course I am, Harry, go on.'

'Well, like I said, he hurt my mom a lot. Just taking off like that without a word to anyone. I was six. Gene was four. I don't like to remember that time. I don't like to talk about it. Later on, there was the divorce and stuff like that, and that was tough, but the worst was at the beginning. Every day I'd get back from school and think: he'll be back today, for sure. Today will be the day. But it never was.'

'That's dreadful. I don't know what to say.'

'That's O.K. We'll talk about something else. I'll tell you a secret if you like.'

'A secret? Great!' Fran smiled.

'But first you've got to turn me over, O.K.? Can you do that, being so little and all?'

'Of course I can. I'm little but tough.' Fran wondered how the words came out at all, what with the rush of feeling that seemed to fill her throat.

'Right,' said Harry. 'You put both arms round my waist and kind of twist and I'll lever myself round with my arms. O.K.?'

Fran nodded. She put both arms around his waist and turned him towards her. His skin was warm from the sun and he smelled. Like what? Air, and water and light and sweat and suntan oil and soap.

'There you go,' she said as she pulled him round. She took her hands away as soon as she could and hugged herself to stop the trembling.

'You're not through yet, kid,' Harry said.

'Slavedriver Harry requires that you oil his back.'

'O.K.' said Fran as lightly as she could. 'Where's the oil?'

'Right there.' Fran rubbed oil into Harry's back, moving her hands in long, smooth strokes. She felt drunk: silence filled her ears, a mist of heat seemed to hang over the house, over the pool. Time didn't exist any more. The whole universe had gathered itself up into these movements, this feeling, Harry's skin under her hands. She felt hypnotised, dazed, she couldn't bring her hands to stop and then... (How did it happen? Later, she would try and reconstruct the exact series of movements, try to slow them and slow them and play them back in her mind, like a video, frame by frame) ... There was a hand behind her head and her mouth was suddenly on Harry's and she was breathing him in, tasting him, smelling the suntan oil, and his hair and then it was over. Fran could think of nothing to say. She looked at the pool, at the house, anywhere but at Harry.

'You're a cute kid, you know that?'

Fran struggled, started to speak and couldn't. She coughed and stood up. In her embarrassment, she put on a false American accent:

'Gee, t'anks!' she said. 'I've got to go now. I want to get a picture of the house, from the front. I'll see you later.'

'What about the secret?' Harry called after her. 'Don't you want to hear it?'

Fran had forgotten all about it, and in view of Harry's behaviour by the pool, didn't much care if she heard it or not. All she wanted to do was to get away by herself somewhere and relive that kiss – the further away the better, but:

'Yes, of course I do. Tell.'

'It's Gene.' Harry said. 'He's nuts about you. Honestly.'

'That's rubbish!' Fran laughed. 'It can't be true, and even if it were true, he'd never tell you.'

'He doesn't have to,' said Harry. 'I'm his brother, remember? I can read his mind.'

Could it be true? Fran felt hot and confused. She had to think. Whatever was she to do now? If Gene loved her, and she loved Harry, and Harry loved – but who did Harry love? Her? Or was it just a friendly, cousinly kiss? It didn't feel like it. It felt like the real thing, although Fran admitted to herself that she hadn't had enough kisses to be able to spot any differences there might be between them. She shook her head. A person could develop a headache from thinking such thoughts in this heat.

'I'm going to get a shot of the front of the house,' she said. 'See you, Harry.'

'O.K.' said Harry, and waved to her as he turned to his book.


## 11.30 a.m. The House. Long Shot

*A large white house set on a grassy slope. Plants grow over the railings of the front porch. There's a row of windows above the porch, and another two windows above that, under the gabled roof. To the right of the house is Grandma Sarah's rose garden. She's been working on it since 1930 and is 'just about getting it into shape.' She still works on it, when she feels good. Just visible behind the house: a corner of the pool. It looks like a chip of aquamarine lying on green velvet.*

Fran was in the kitchen, whipping cream for the strawberry shortcake: Grandpa's favourite and the final touch to a meal that seemed to have been in preparation for days. Susan, Rose and Jean had undertaken to put it together, but it looked to Fran as if Jean were doing most of the work, and the others were just gossiping, to each other and to her.

Susan said: 'If Mike had lived it would have been our thirty-fifth wedding anniversary this year,' and sighed as she licked a spoon. 'Did I tell you how we met? My sisters laugh at me, honey, but I reckon it's the most romantic thing. Mike rang up my boss, see, for something or other one day and I answered the phone, being his secretary. And he didn't say a thing to me, but when he'd finished his business with my boss, he said:'

' "Tell that secretary of yours that she's the woman I'm going to mary!" ' chorused Rose and Jean, and started laughing.

'Gee, Sue,' Rose said 'I wish I had a dollar for each time you told that story!'

Jean just shook her head. Susan looked thwarted, sulky, like a small child. She turned to Fran. 'Don't pay them no mind, they're just jealous. Nothing that romantic ever happened to them, is all.'

Rose smiled slyly, and began arranging plump strawberries on eiderdowns of fluffy cream. 'You saying my Bill isn't romantic, Sue? Well, I guess you're right at that. He isn't. But he's steady.

118

There's a lot to be said for reliability. Even predictability. I know where I am with Bill.'

Jean, with her back to her sisters, took the empty cream bowl from Fran and winked at her and whispered. 'Dullsville... that's where she is with Bill. And she knows it, too.'

'I hear you whispering there,' Sue cried. 'Little Jeannie with the light brown hair! What're you whispering about?'

'Fran's telling me all her secrets,' said Jean.

'No, I wasn't...' Fran began.

'She's kidding,' said Rose. 'Jean always kids everyone. We reckon that's why she never married. Never did seem to take anyone seriously. Don't let the way she dresses fool you, Fran. Not for a minute. That's just a front...'

'Rose! Just because you spend your days all gussied up, doesn't mean that everyone...'

'Gussied up, she says. Sue, did you hear that?'

'Cut it out, will you?' Sue, the eldest sister, placed small rosebuds round the cake. It occurred to Fran that she had probably been saying the same to Rose and Jean for half a century. 'You're behaving like a couple of kids – bickering...'

'Who's bickering?' said Patti, coming into the kitchen. 'Why, that is a cake of cakes! Wait till they see that. Seems almost too good to eat. Maybe Fran can take a photograph of it, so that we never forget it. What do you say, Fran?'

'Yes,' said Fran, 'only I want you, too. All of you. Could you stand behind the cake?'

'Right,' said Patti. 'Shall I sit right here, behind it?' She smiled as her sisters-in-law gathered around her.

119

Fran took the photograph.

## 2.00 p.m. The Kitchen. Patti, Susan, Rose, Jean and the Strawberry Shortcake

*On the whorls and lines of the scrubbed pine table, a blue plate holding a skyscraper of a cake: four golden shortcake circles, four snowdrifts of cream, strawberries like spots of blood just visible. Around the base of the cake, pink rosebuds and green leaves. At the other end of the table, Patti sits, and her husband's sisters lean over her shoulders and put their faces near hers so that the eye of the camera can see them all, catch them all, laughing. Happy that the cake has turned out so well. Sixty years married to the same person calls for a cake like this, their eyes say. Patti and Joe will perhaps live to deserve this kind of a cake, but it's too late for Susan and Jean and as for Rose: who can tell?*

'What're you wearing tonight, child?' Grandma Sarah, sitting in the rocking chair on the porch looked every inch the pretty old lady Fran had seen rocking on similar porches in a dozen movies.

'My best dress, of course,' said Fran, 'but you'll be the belle of the ball.'

Grandma Sarah laughed. 'I always was, you know. Didn't Mary tell you that?'

Fran took a moment to realize that Grandma Sarah was speaking of her own Great-grandmother, now dead. 'Yes, she did, of course. And showed me photographs.'

Grandma Sarah sighed. 'Things would've been quite different now if only . . .'

'If only what?'

'If only I hadn't set my cap at Grandpa. He was Mary's beau, you know. I figure that was why she upped and ran away to England. Poor Mary. I guess it wasn't a kind thing to do, but if you'd seen him in those days... Lordy, Lordy, what a man!' Grandma Sarah rocked backwards and forwards and closed her eyes. 'Harry has the look of him. I can see him all over again.'

Fran tried to make the connection. Harry? Golden Harry and the wrinkled, shrivelled old man in the loud print shirts: the same? Would Harry look like that? Ever? She couldn't believe it.

'You not saying a thing, eh?' Grandma Sarah chuckled. 'You've got it bad, I guess. Am I right?'

'I don't know what you mean, Grandma Sarah.'

'I mean Harry. You fancy you're in love with him. I don't blame you honey. Only watch yourself.'

'You and Grandpa seem O.K.' Fran decided not to deny it. 'Sixty years together and everything.'

'Don't let that fool you, Fran. It's no picnic, being married to a man who's like some kind of candle.'

'I don't understand – why a candle?'

'They burn so bright that all the moths around just can't help it they keep coming near and getting burned.'

'Moths?' Fran was finding herself more and more confused.

'Other women.' Grandma Sarah paused. 'They never stop trying to get close. And they succeed, too, sometimes. They get their wings singed in the end, but some of them... well, they get – they stick

121

around for a while. It's no picnic. Don't let the sixty years baloney blind you to that. It's not been one long bed of roses, no sir.'

Fran understood at last. 'But it's you he loves,' she said. 'Isn't it? Here you are together after all those years. Aren't you happy?'

'Sure I'm happy now, child. There's no one going to steal him away now!' She smiled. 'But you watch yourself with Harry. He's the same. A candle, if ever I saw one.'

Grandma Sarah closed her eyes and before long Fran could tell from her even breathing, she was asleep. The camera was on the table beside her. Fran picked it up and took a shot of her great-grandmother's sister as she lay in the rocking chair.

## 3.45 p.m. Close-up. Grandma Sarah

*The white back of the rocking chair is like a halo round Grandma Sarah's white hair. The wrinkles are there, and the grey hair, but so is the delicate nose, and the fine mouth and the soft curves of cheek and brow. And Grandma Sarah is slim. Not as supple as she used to be when she was young, of course not. But much the same shape. Only her feet really betray her. She is wearing slippers over toes that are gnarled and bent like tiny tree roots. Fran saw them once, although they are generally hidden away. Grandma Sarah prefers to remember them as they were: tucked out of sight in satin pumps with diamanté buckles and thin heels. She wears a wedding ring and no other jewellery, although she has plenty, upstairs in her bedroom. She no longer has on the lace blouse she wore for the Family Group. The high neck must have been stifling in this weather. She has changed into cream slacks and a loose cotton top the colour of the wistaria that droops over the roof of the porch and casts a shadow over her hands, clasped unmoving in her lap.*


Gene and Fran were riding slowly back to the house.

'I don't know why I agreed to this ride,' Fran said. 'It's too hot. Why didn't we stay by the pool?'

'I dunno,' said Gene. 'I like getting out of there sometimes, going off somewhere. It gets to be a bit... demanding, especially today. We'd have been sucked in if we'd stuck around. To lay the table or put up the bunting or string fairy lights all over the porch or something.'

'Maybe we should have helped...' Fran began.

'We'll say we were being considerate, getting out from under their feet... it's O.K. Don't worry about it.'

'Can we stop for air?' Fran said. 'I need a breather. Is there any Coke left?'

'It'll be hot, though,' said Gene. 'After sitting in the basket for so long.'

'That's O.K. I'm used to it,' said Fran. 'Cokes are always warm in England.'

'Is that right?' Gene laughed. 'Sounds a real weird place. The more you tell me about it the weirder it sounds.'

'The beer is warm too,' Fran said.

'You kidding me? Boy, am I glad we got our Independence!'

They sat down by the side of the road in the shade of a tree and drank in silence. Fran lay back on the grass and closed her eyes. When Gene spoke, his voice seemed to come to her from a distance.

'Hey, Fran,' he said. 'When you go back there, to that weird England of yours...' he stopped.

'Yes?'

'Well, will you write back to me?'

'Would you write back?'

'Sure I would.'

Fran sat up and looked at Gene, who was staring out at the road with his back to her. She said: 'You don't look like a letter writer to me.'

'Don't think I ever wrote a letter in my life before, but I'd write to you.'

Fran smiled. Since Harry had told her of Gene's feelings for her, a lot of the things Gene had said over the days had fallen into a recognisable shape. She had thought he was simply being friendly, but now she understood. What she had difficulty in understanding was her own reaction. She felt – there was only one word for it – powerful. As if she could ask Gene for whatever she wanted and he would give it to her, as though she were a magnet, drawing him. It was quite a pleasant sensation, and she wondered if this was how Harry felt all the time, towards everyone, and how she would behave in his place. Thinking about all this made her feel dizzy: a word from her could hurt Gene. If he knew how she felt about his brother, what would he say? Do? I don't want to hurt him, he's too nice, she thought. He *is* nice. He's not even bad-looking, though he's not Harry, but he's a boy. He's six months younger than me, and small and thin, so he looks even younger. And Harry... Harry's a man.

'Yes,' she said. 'Of course I'll write to you. I'm a very good letter writer, as it happens. You'll keep

me up to date with all the family news, O.K.?'
(Harry's news – lots of that.)

'You want bulletins about Grandma Sarah's rose garden and Susan's latest diet and you want to know if Jean elopes with the bank manager and runs away to Venezuela, that kind of thing?'

'Just news. You know.'

'Right. I guess I could cope with that.'

'Anyway, I'm not leaving till Thursday. That's four days still.'

'Don't remind me.'

'Why not?' (Oh, this awful power, making her do it. Making her want to crack open Gene's secret and find his feeling for her, wanting him to tell her . . . Why? What was she going to do if he did say something? Would she tell him about Harry? What? How?)

Gene considered the question. 'Because I'll miss you. It's been so great having you here. Showing you things – just doing things together.'

Fran felt a sudden wave of affection and tenderness rush over her. She wanted to ruffle his hair and hug him to her as if he were her child.

She said: 'I've had fun too, Gene. Really. And of course I'll miss you.' She took his hand and gave it a squeeze.

'Fran . . .' His voice shook. 'Do you have a boyfriend or something, in England?'

I should say yes, Fran thought. I should lie. I really should. It would get me out of the situation so neatly. Lie, go on, lie.

'No,' said Fran. 'There's no one in England.'

'Then can I go ahead and kiss you?'

Fran laughed. 'I don't know. Are you supposed

125

to ask? Is that how it's done?'

'I guess the usual way is, you fall into my arms and it just kind of happens, like in the movies, without a word being said. But I don't seem to get into those kinds of situations. So I've got to ask you, Fran. Do you mind?'

'What? The asking or the kissing?' (Stop, she cried out to herself, stop tormenting him! Look how anxious he looks. Oh, Gene, I don't want to hurt you.)

She put her arm around his shoulder and he turned to her. She closed her eyes. Gene was trembling as he kissed her. She could feel the bones of his shoulders through the hot cotton of his T-shirt, trembling.

Afterwards he said: 'I can't think of a word to say, which is unusual for me.'

'We'd better go back now,' Fran said. 'I bet they will want us to lay the table or something.'

They got on to the bicycles and rode along in silence. Then Gene said: 'Know what I want to do?'

'What?'

'I want to go back and lock myself in my room and play those few seconds back there over and over again, like some kind of video in my head.'

'Why, that's . . .' Fran bit her lip. That's how she felt, she'd been going to say. This morning with Harry. Tonight, she'd sit between Harry and Gene and not know where to put herself. If only I were at home, she thought suddenly, far away from all of them. She'd never realized living in Paradise would have such problems. On the other hand, she reasoned, all the others would be there. I won't be alone with either of them. I'll worry what to do tomorrow. Tonight I'm going to enjoy the party.

'I'll put the bikes away,' Gene said as they approached the garage.

'Can I take a photo of you first?' said Fran. 'Just standing by the bike?'

'O.K.' Gene struck a pose. 'Like this?'

'No,' said Fran. 'Just normal, please.'

'You got it,' he said and grinned, just as Fran pressed the button.

## 5 p.m. Close-up. Gene.

*His faded blue T-shirt hangs outside his jeans. It is none too clean. Neither are the jeans. There are holes at the knees. On his feet he wears trainers that used once to be white. He has pushed back the silky fringe of light brown hair that usually falls over his face and left a dirty mark on his forehead in the process. But his teeth are white and straight, and the bike is gleaming. Gene may not take great pains with his own appearance, but it's clear he lavishes all the time and attention in the world on anything he cares about.*

Fran looked at herself in the mirror and hardly recognised the image that shone back at her.

'Is that me?' she asked Eleanor. 'I can't believe it. Thank you so much. You wouldn't think just putting up a few strands of hair and twisting it this way and that could make such a difference. I feel grown-up.' She sighed with satisfaction and turned to Eleanor, who bent down and hugged her.

'You look real pretty, Fran. That's a lovely dress too.'

127

'I don't look as pretty as you. I never will.'

'Why, that's the nicest thing anyone's said to me for the longest time. I love my boys to bits, but you know, I wish I had a girl sometimes. I really miss not having a daughter.'

'And I wish...' Fran stopped. She had been about to say: 'I wish I had a mother like you, who'd put my hair up in loops and spirals and lend me her pearl necklace for parties,' but a sense of guilty loyalty to her own mother prevented her. What would she be doing tonight? Sitting on the old sofa in her rust-coloured cardigan and reading the Sunday papers? Watching television?

'Mom!' came a shout from just outside the door. Harry. 'You in there? Can I come in?'

Eleanor looked at Fran, who nodded. Without waiting for permission Harry burst in, pushing his wheelchair across the carpet at high speed.

'Mom, guess who phoned? Ronnie– can you believe it? And she's here. She just got back. Anyway, I asked Patti, and she said O.K. why not, and so I asked her to come over tonight for the party. Isn't that great? Isn't that fantastic?' Without waiting for an answer, he turned the wheelchair round and glided out of the room.

Fran turned back to face the mirror. The image that had pleased her so much only moments before now disgusted her. Harry didn't look at her, didn't even see her. He was taken up with this Ronnie. Who was she? Why had no one mentioned her? And how dare she just turn up like this and muscle in on a family occasion?

'That's wonderful for Harry,' Eleanor said. 'He and Ronnie are so fond of each other.'

128

'Is she his girlfriend?' Fran forced her voice into a kind of steadiness. Eleanor laughed.

'Harry has girlfriends like other guys have shirts. One for each day of the week. But Ronnie's special to him, I guess. Wait till you see her. You'll see why.'

Fran struggled not to cry. If she cried, her mascara would run. If she cried, everyone would know. She felt a moment of pure loathing for pretty, unconcerned Eleanor, who was clever about hair and make-up and so stupid she couldn't see how Fran felt about her son.

'I'd better go down now and help with the table,' she said.

'Just wait one second,' said Eleanor. 'I'm going to take a photo of you right now, just as you are. You look so terrific.' She picked up the camera from Fran's bedside table. 'Sit where you are, right there on the stool and look up at me. That's it.'

Eleanor focused on Fran's face and pressed the button.

'Hey, will you look at that!' she cried. 'I'm in the shot as well. In the mirror. Gee, Fran honey, I'm sorry. Why didn't I think of that?'

'It doesn't matter, honestly,' Fran said. 'Actually, I think it looks interesting like that.'

'You're being polite,' Eleanor smiled. 'I guess that's because you're British.'

*7.00 p.m. Close-up. Fran, with Eleanor.*

*The lamp on the dressing-table has edged Fran's hair with gold. Her eyes are shadowed and she is unsmiling. The silky material of her dress falls over her shoulders in folds of*

129

*scarlet and the pearls round her neck shine from the warmth
of her skin. Behind her in the mirror you can see Eleanor,
taking the photograph. Her red hair falls over the camera.
Her dress is made of chiffon: turquoise, blue, green, mauve
blending in an ocean of colour. Also reflected are the wall-
lights above Eleanor's head: small, cream lampshades
fringed with tassels. A field of soft, pink carpet stretches
away to the door.*

'I don't think,' said Susan 'I'm ever going to eat
another morsel as long as I live.'

Gene bent towards Fran and whispered: 'Five'll
get you ten she'll have buckwheat pancakes for
breakfast. Wait and see.'

Fran giggled. She had been giggling a lot: from
the sea-food salad, through the turkey-with-all-the-
trimmings, right up to the strawberry shortcake. It
must be the wine, she thought vaguely. She looked
at Gene, beside her. She looked at Harry and
Ronnie sitting right across the table from her.
Ronnie. When she'd first met her before dinner,
about a hundred years ago, Fran felt the shock of
recognition. Ronnie was the female equivalent of
Harry. Miss Golden. She and Harry fitted like two
halves of a torn dollar bill. Look at the way she
dressed! A black and white pinstriped suit, like a
Chicago gangster (in June, for goodness sake!) with
a black and white checked shirt. Stripes and checks
together – the daring of it took Fran's breath away.
Ronnie had straight, blond hair, cut like a boy's, a
wide mouth and a skin like all the words in all the
make-up advertisements in the world. Fran drank

wine, all the wine she was offered to blur the truth which she knew and couldn't bear. This Ronnie, whoever she was, was Something Else. A different league. Almost a different species from herself. She turned to Gene for consolation.

'Isn't Ronnie lovely?' she whispered.

Gene considered. He took a bit of seafood salad and swallowed it. 'She's O.K.' he said. 'If you like the Robert Redford type.'

That's when Fran started giggling. Everyone ate too much. There was too much talk. Reminiscences. Fran listened and giggled and looked around. The strawberry shortcake was in ruins: crumbs and blobby bits of cream lay about on the plate, and the rosebuds had long ago fallen off on to the white lace of Grandma Sarah's best tablecloth.

'I think I'm drunk,' Fran said to Gene. 'I'm seeing things.'

'What things?'

'I can't describe it – it's strange.' For a moment, or maybe for longer, Fran had felt as if she were a long way away, up on the ceiling, perhaps and looking down on to the table. The people had vanished and only their clothes were left: clothes sitting up in chairs. There was Rose's black lace, leaning over to talk to Joe's tuxedo. Susan's yellow dress billowed over the table. Jean's wine-coloured silk and Patti's beige, Eleanor's sea-coloured chiffon and Grandma Sarah's lavender velvet, draped themselves this way and that. And the arm of Harry's jacket was around the shoulders of a Chicago gangster suit in black and white stripes, right across the table from a red silk dress that was sitting up very straight in its chair.

'Fran honey, where's that magic box of yours?' Grandpa looked down the table at her.

'I'll get it, Grandpa,' said Fran. 'It's in my bedroom.'

'It's O.K.' said Gene. 'I'll get it. You'll fall over if you try and get up.'

'I won't,' said Fran weakly, but Gene had gone.

When he returned there was a debate about who should take the picture. Back and forth the talk went, over the crumbs and the patterns in the tablecloth. In the end Fran spoke:

'Listen, Grandpa,' she said. 'It's my camera and I'm taking this picture. So there.' The wine had given her courage. She stood, rather unsteadily at the end of the table and looked at them all. They were smiling.

'Watch the birdie,' she said.

*10.30 p.m. The Dining Room, Anniversary Dinner.*

*Everyone is smiling. What does it mean? Grandpa's smile says: I made it. I'm eighty-four and still here and so's Sarah, and these are my children and my grandchildren and great-grandchildren and even a branch of the family tree from England, flown over specially for the occasion, like a florist's delivery. Grandma Sarah's smile is wistful. I'm a good-looking old lady, it says, sure, but for how much longer? She seems to be glancing at Ronnie as if at her own past. Susan's smile is brave – her corset is pinching like hell. Rose's is a little forced. She is smiling at Bill, who smiles obediently back at her. Jean is enigmatic as usual, a Mona Lisa smile. Eleanor grins proudly, and so she should, looking at her sons. Harry smiles at Ronnie. Possessively.*

132

*She looks happy, happy with herself and with Harry, and with good reason. Gene is smiling straight at the camera. Or, and this is more likely, at the person holding the camera. He is smiling at Fran and his eyes look as if they're pleased with what they're seeing.*

'It's O.K. Fran, honey. Honest, it's O.K. Really.' Gene was pleading. 'You don't have to cry. You don't have to feel bad about it. It's nothing to be ashamed of. You just had too much to drink, that's all. I've cleaned up after people before. At camp and even right here – why, I clean up after Harry all the time...'

Fran burst into fresh paroxysms of tears. 'Don't tell Harry,' she begged. 'Please don't tell Harry I threw up. I couldn't bear it.'

Gene looked at her, puzzled. 'I won't if you don't want me to. But it beats me why not. You O.K now? Come on into the kitchen and I'll get you a cup of coffee.'

'My head hurts,' said Fran.

'Sure it does. Hurt even worse in the morning. You wait.'

'That's terrific. You certainly know how to cheer a person up.'

'I'm just a little ray of sunshine. Didn't you know? C'mon.'

In the kitchen, they drank coffee sitting at the table. 'I still get a kick staying up late, d'you know that?' Gene said. 'I guess it means I'm not an adult yet.'

'I feel as if I could sleep for a week.' She paused.

'Gene, I want to tell you something.'

'Shoot.'

'Back there, it wasn't just the food and the drink, you know . . . it was something I saw. I shouldn't tell you really, only I must speak about it. I'm sorry, Gene. You see, I went out to sit by the pool, just to get a bit of air and I suppose I was feeling a bit drunk and then . . .'

'Go on.'

'Well,' Fran gulped at her coffee. 'Harry and Ronnie were out there. They were . . . well, kissing. I mean, they didn't even see me or hear me they were so taken up with one another. I just fled. I couldn't look.'

'That made you throw up? Seriously? You mean because of Harry? You figured I didn't know what you felt about him? You're crazy, Fran. It sticks out a mile. I knew before you did, I guess.'

'Didn't it bother you? After – well, I mean, I thought you liked me and everything.'

'No percentage being jealous of Harry any more than being jealous of a flower or the Grand Canyon or something like that. Any way, I'm an optimist. I reckoned after you kissed me, I'd quit being a frog and turn into a prince for you, right there on the spot.'

Fran laughed. 'This morning you were an Ugly Duckling.'

'And you said I'd turn into a swan eventually.' Gene stood up and pirouetted round the floor. 'How'm I doing?'

'I like you so much, Gene,' Fran said, 'you're so nice and funny and kind . . .'

' . . . and handsome and clever. Go on. Don't stop there.'

134

Fran looked down at her empty coffee cup. She said: 'I want to explain about Harry. I thought this morning that I loved him, but I can see it now – it wasn't love. It was more like being dazzled... It wasn't altogether real. I can't explain it. It was like a picture of love, a dream of it, a sort of fantasy on my part. I mean, this whole place doesn't seem like the real world to me. It's difficult for an American to understand, I know, but for me and for a lot of people who've never been here, the whole place is like a movie we carry round in our heads. Or a hundred different movies: western plains, city streets, beaches full of surfers, Southern plantations. Everything. And Harry's part of that. All tied up with that. Even this house and all of you, even though you're family, seem – I don't know. Remote from my ordinary life. When I'm here, I find it difficult to think about school, and my own little bedroom and the small square of grass that's my garden.'

'What about me? Am I a dream, too?' Gene asked quietly.

'No, you're real. You're the only one of the whole lot of them I can picture coming down to the chip shop with me. Riding on the bus to school with me...'

'I'll do that!' Gene's face lit up. 'Next summer. You wait. I'll be over there, wait and see, and we'll ride all the buses you like and you can feed me warm Cokes. I won't care. I mean it. I'm coming. You expect me. O.K?'

Fran smiled in spite of herself. 'How can you be so sure?'

'Well, now, you see. It's a family tradition. Seventeen years old, you get a ticket to Europe.

Grandpa practically insists. Only I'm going to skip all that art galleries and cathedrals jazz and just concentrate on England. I can't wait.'

'It'll be wonderful if it happens.' Fran yawned.

Gene said: 'It will. I promise...' and then the door opened and Jean came in and grinned at them.

'You kids still up? Do you know what time it is? Look at you. You look a real mess, both of you. Bed. Right now.'

'Aw, Jean, c'mon. I don't feel like sleeping – hey, do you realize we have the same name? I feel like I'm talking to myself...' Gene laughed and whispered to Fran: 'Tomorrow night I'll take you to a drive-in movie.' He put his arm around her shoulders and pulled her towards him, whispered in her ear: 'You know. We'll kiss so much, we won't see much of what's going on. It's a real Old American Cliché. You'll just love it!'

'Are you kids through fooling around?' Jean said. 'I'm supposed to be locking up around here.'

Fran giggled and clung to Gene. 'Will you take a photo of us, please?' she said.

Jean laughed. 'You must be out of your mind, Fran. Have you seen what you look like? Whoever takes photos at two in the morning anyway?

'Please, Jean, it's very important.'

'If it's going to get you guys out of the kitchen, I'll do anything. Go on, then. Smile or something.'

Gene and Fran smiled at one another.

*2.00 a.m. Close-up. Fran and Gene.*

*Fran's hair has come down. All the party spirals and curls*

136

are hanging round her shoulders. Gene has the sleeves of his evening shirt turned up above the elbows. Also, his tie has disappeared. The shirt is open at the neck. One hand is in Fran's hair, lifting it up a little. Fran looks pale, but she is smiling and so is Gene. No one would know that they'd asked for this picture to be taken. It's as though the photographer didn't exist, as though the camera has caught them off guard just at that moment. Seeing one another properly for the very first time. Knowing.

# WILLIAM GILMOUR

## THE CLUB: HELLO, AMERICA!

**If your brother died on tour, would you join the same band?**

John nearly hadn't auditioned but now here he was on his way to America, the new guitarist for The Messengers. The playing side he could do easily. But could he keep his identity a secret? And would he be able to find out how his brother really died?

**Hello, America! We're back . . .**

**LIGHTNING**

**JEAN RICHARDSON**
Editor


BEWARE! BEWARE!


Beware, beware the nine chilling tales within these covers... Spine tingling words from the pens of Peter Dickinson, Jane Gardam, Berlie Doherty and others.

Can you bear the suspense of reading them? Beware! Beware...


**LIGHTNING**

## ALSO BY CHRISTOPHER PIKE

### CHAIN LETTER

*THEY ALL SHARED THE SAME SECRET...*
*NOW THEY WOULD SHARE THE SAME*
*TERROR*

When Alison first read the chain letter signed
'Your Caretaker', she thought it was some
terrible sick joke. Someone, somewhere knew
about that awful night when she and six other
friends committed an unthinkable crime in the
desolate California desert. And now that person
was determined to make them pay for it.

One by one, the chain letter was coming to each
of them... demanding dangerous, impossible
deeds... threatening violence if the demands
were not met. No one out of the seven wanted to
believe that this nightmare was really happening to them. Until the accidents started
happening – and the dying...

### LIGHTNING